*The*

# Mystery
*of*
# Raspberry
# Hill

EVA FRANTZ is a Finnish radio and TV presenter and author. She was already an award-winning writer of crime novels for grown-ups when she wrote *The Mystery of Raspberry Hill*, her first book for children, which won the prestigious Runeberg Junior Prize. Although set in Finland, this book was actually inspired by a visit to Hampton Court Palace in London, which is said to be haunted by many ghosts.

A.A. PRIME is an award-winning translator from Swedish to English. Her previous translations for Pushkin Children's include Maria Turtschaninoff's *Red Abbey Chronicles* trilogy.

# The
# Mystery
## of
# Raspberry
# Hill

## EVA FRANTZ

TRANSLATED FROM THE SWEDISH
BY A.A. PRIME

PUSHKIN CHILDREN'S

Pushkin Press
65–69 Shelton Street
London WC2H 9HE

*The Mystery of Raspberry Hill* was first published as
*Hallonbacken* by Schildts & Söderströms in Helsinki, 2018

First published by Pushkin Press in 2022

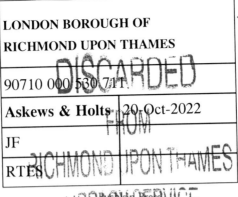

FINNISH
LITERATURE
EXCHANGE

This work has been published with the financial
assistance of FILI - Finnish Literature Exchange

1 3 5 7 9 8 6 4 2

ISBN 13: 978-1-78269-341-3

Designed and typeset by Tetragon, London

Printed and bound by Clays Ltd, Elcograf S.p.A.

www.pushkinpress.com

*The*

# Mystery
*of*
# Raspberry
# Hill

# I

# The Motor Car

My name is Stina and I'm probably going to die soon. No one has told me so, but I'm no fool. I see it in Mama's eyes. I hear the neighbourhood women murmur and mutter. They tilt their heads and cluck their tongues when they see me. *Tut-tut-tut.*

Sometimes I hear them whisper too.

"Poor Märta, first her husband and now her little girl."

Märta is my mother. My father's name was Paul but he's dead now. He was killed in the war. The war is over, but that doesn't make Papa any less dead. And soon I'll be dead as well. I cough and I cough, sometimes so hard that the bedsheets get all bloody.

It's those times especially when Mama's eyes grow dark and awfully sad.

But when you know that death is coming soon, you take every opportunity to enjoy things to the fullest. Like getting to ride in a motor car! I never dreamt I would get the chance to do such a thing, but now I have! And what an elegant motor car it was! Red and gleaming. The seats were soft and tan, made of leather, I think. The other kids back home on Sjömansgatan could hardly believe their eyes when it stopped right outside our front door and a man wearing a uniform with shiny buttons asked which one of us was Stina.

It was the kind of motor car that rich, important people travel around in. Film stars and politicians. So it seemed rather special that I, Stina from Sjömansgatan, a consumptive little urchin, was allowed to get in. I felt like Greta Garbo.

On the seat next to me I had my little brown travel bag. It contained almost everything I own. Which isn't much. A few well-worn garments, my doll Rosa, a spinning top made for me by Peter from the market hall, two litho prints (one of an angel with pinkish wings, the other of two hands, a man's and a woman's, holding each other inside a flower wreath), and a photograph of Papa and Mama. They look very young and serious in the picture. Hard to believe they had the money to go to a photographer back then before they got engaged.

I wonder if I'll ever be photographed in my life. My time is running out...

The greatest treasure in my bag was wrapped in my nightdress so it wouldn't get dog-eared during the journey. I can hardly believe that I am now the owner of such a beautiful book! *Robinson Crusoe* is the title and it actually belongs to my big brother Olle. I was sitting on the doorstep ready to go, with my hair plaited and cardigan buttoned up, waiting to be taken away, when he appeared all of a sudden and handed it to me.

"Here, Stina, this is for you," he said and walked away.

This book is Olle's most beloved possession, I'm sure of it. More than once I'd asked if I might leaf through, even just to take a glance at the pictures, but he always said no and acted very protective of it. And then he gave it to me, just like that!

I guess Olle knows that I'm going to die soon. I'll make sure he gets *Robinson Crusoe* back when I do. I could write a will. That's what Grandma Josefa did before she died. It was a good thing too, because otherwise Papa wouldn't have had a wedding ring to give Mama. Grandma was very well prepared and wrote on a piece of paper that Paul should get the ring, so it all worked out. Wills are important—I mustn't forget to write mine before I die.

The man driving the car asked if I wanted to lie down across the seats and rest. But my cough becomes much worse when I lie down so I asked if I might sit upright. Besides, you simply must look out the window when travelling by motor car, especially if you're unlikely to ever have the chance again.

We had a long way to go. The sanatorium is deep inside the forest where the air is pure and healthy. Usually only rich people go to such fancy sanatoriums, so it's pretty incredible that I've been given the opportunity as well.

It was a few weeks ago now that Dr Lundin came to our home and asked what Mama would say about sending little Stina away to stay in a sanatorium for a time. He was actually asking on behalf of another doctor who was an old friend.

At Raspberry Hill Sanatorium they wanted to research what happened when city kids with bad coughs spent time out in the countryside. Would the fresh air alone be enough to cure them? That's what the doctors thought. They wanted to test it out on me, and study me and my lungs to see if I got better from being at the sanatorium.

Personally, I didn't believe it for a second. How could ordinary air help? There's air everywhere already.

I had got a lot worse over the summer. Back in spring I could still walk down to the harbour with Olle and Edith to watch the boats go by and fetch firewood for Mama. I could feed the chickens and help with the mangle on Mondays. I fetched drinking water from the water post nearly every day. I could walk to school too. But then I started coughing and never stopped. I'd been lying in the kitchen and coughing for so long, seeing nothing of the outside world except the little courtyard outside our building. So just imagine how exciting it was to suddenly be whisked away through the streets of Helsinki in a film star car, and driven past fields, hills, forests and lakes. I turned my head this way and that until my neck ached.

Mama didn't want me to go to Raspberry Hill at first, and neither did I. But then she dared to hope—what if I really could be cured at the sanatorium?

Wouldn't it be madness to turn down such an opportunity?

I think it was the neighbourhood women who convinced her.

"But dear Märta, think how much easier it would be on you. The girl would be taken care of and you could see to your other five."

Yes, that's right. Six children and no father. All the others are healthy and help Mama out as much as they can.

Olle is fourteen already and has been working as an errand boy, but he's looking for a job at the harbour now. Sailing is what he really wants to do. Edith is thirteen and helps Mama on busy days when she has more shirt collars dropped off than she can iron by herself. My younger siblings, twins Lars and Ellen, and little Erik who was still in Mama's belly when Papa was killed in action, are all big enough to help out around the house. But I am no use. I am frail, I cough and get in the way. Plus everyone was afraid that I might be contagious, so my siblings all had to sleep together in the bedroom while Mama and I slept in the kitchen.

They will have a lot more space now that I'm gone. I understand what a relief it must be for

Mama not to have me around, even though she's sad about it too.

It's probably just as well that they get used to me not being there, because that's how it will be when I'm dead.

Mama spent the evenings before I left knitting. She got the yarn from unpicking outgrown jumpers and socks. She sat there by the fire, knitting and knitting, and sometimes she would look up from her needles and let out a deep sigh. Then she would carry on.

She probably didn't realize I was awake and watching her. I wanted to watch her very closely so I wouldn't forget what she looked like when I was at the sanatorium. She is beautiful, my mother. She has dark hair and blue eyes, just like me. We are both thin, but Mama has rounder cheeks and pink lips. My lips are so pale they are practically invisible. Mama almost always has her hair tied in a bun, but occasionally at the bathhouse I have seen it all loose and curly. Then I think she looks like a queen from a fairy tale. I wish I had hair like that, but mine is dead straight and quite fine. Several women on our block have their hair cut short. It's modern and practical, they say. But I hope Mama never cuts her queenly hair.

On my last night at home on Sjömansgatan I received a package. Inside was a newly knitted cardigan! An oddball sort of cardigan that changes colour here and there whenever the yarn runs out, but still the most beautiful cardigan I've ever seen! It was the first time I had ever been given a new garment of my own, and not a hand-me-down from Edith, or sometimes even from Olle. If I bury my nose into the collar I can smell Mama's scent. I am going to wear it every day at the sanatorium.

## 2

# The Castle in the Woods

I will never forget the first time I laid eyes on Raspberry Hill Sanatorium. I must have fallen asleep in the motor car because I was woken up when we took a sudden turn onto a narrower road.

We were driving along an avenue lined with large, old trees. Oak, I think. We drove past a gleaming lake, then up a steep hill, and there it was.

I had never seen such a massive building, not even back in the city! Or did it only seem so big because it was surrounded by nothing but forest? Like a castle! Four storeys, turrets and balconies, round windows and ornate doors. There wasn't time to count all the windows on the facade, but it must have been over a hundred!

Back home, seven of us lived in two small rooms, but I imagined Raspberry Hill could probably house thousands without ever getting crowded! There were only two people to be seen, though. They were standing on the wide steps leading up to the front door, both dressed in white.

The motor car stopped and the driver got out and opened the door for me.

"Here you are, miss, we've arrived."

All of a sudden I felt shy and childish, not at all like a film star, as I slipped off the seat and climbed out of the car clutching my travel bag. I remembered to straighten my skirt and pull up my knee socks before curtsying to the two people in white. We may be poor, but manners cost nothing, as Mama always says.

The two women standing on the steps wore identical nurse uniforms. Other than that they couldn't have been more different. One was young and rotund with rosy cheeks. A few wisps of curly fair hair stuck out from under her cap. When she smiled dimples appeared in her cheeks, like I've always wished I had. But you can't have dimples in a face as skinny as mine, it would just look strange. The other woman was tall and thin and had dark hair in a low, tight bun. She was the elder of the two and looked at me sternly, as if I had just done something very naughty.

The fair one spoke first.

"Little Stina, I presume? How was your journey?"

"Fine thanks," I mumbled and curtsied again.

"I'm Sister Petronella and this is the chief nurse of Raspberry Hill, Sister Emerentia."

I curtsied a third time to be on the safe side. Sister Emerentia eyed me grimly but then lowered her neck in a minuscule nod that I supposed to be a greeting of sorts.

"Come with me and I'll take you up to the ward," said Sister Petronella. "I can carry your bag."

Sister Petronella took my hand as we walked up the steps and into the building. We entered through large heavy wooden doors with green windows and came into a vast foyer. There were patterned stone tiles on the floor and the walls were painted light green with little flourishes all over. I had never seen anything like it—it seemed like a train station and a church combined. Only much bigger.

Wide corridors extended to the right and left of us and looked as though they went on for ever. Straight ahead, a large grey staircase with twirly iron railings snaked up several storeys. I tried to tilt my head back enough to see the ceiling all the way at the top of the stairs but almost tripped over my own feet.

"This way," said Sister Petronella.

We managed to walk up a few steps before I had to stop and cough. Sister Petronella waited patiently before we carried on.

The building almost seemed bigger from the inside. Yet there wasn't a soul to be seen, except one other nurse who passed by on the first floor pushing a small trolley.

"Are there a lot of patients living here?" I asked.

"Not many," answered Sister Petronella. "But more are coming all the time, now that things are back to normal again after the fire."

"There was a fire here?"

"Oh yes, didn't Miss Stina know? The whole East Wing burned down a few years ago. The sanatorium had to be closed. But we're back now."

She smiled proudly, but the thought of it gave me a shiver. Fire is my worst fear. There was a fire on Munkholmen Island once when I was little. Olle and Edith and I stood on the rocks watching on. Some people couldn't escape in time and... no, it was too awful.

"Sister Petronella..."

"Yes?"

"Did anyone die in the fire?"

Sister Petronella's dimples disappeared.

"Don't trouble yourself about it, Miss Stina. No reason to give yourself nightmares. Everything is fine now and Raspberry Hill is the best, most advanced sanatorium in all of Europe, don't you know? You should count yourself very lucky to be here!"

I started coughing again and we had to wait until I had finished. How long did we have to go on walking? It felt like we had already been walking down this same corridor for several minutes.

"Here we are, Ward Fourteen!" Sister Petronella said, cheery again, and came to a halt.

She opened the door to a room, or should I say a large hall. Almost everything inside was snow white. The walls were white, the ceiling was white, even the sky outside was white instead of blue. There were eight tightly-made beds in two rows and white curtains hanging from the ceiling.

All the beds were empty.

"Now you can choose whichever bed you like, Miss Stina!"

"But... am I the only one who's going to sleep here?"

"That's right. Like I said, we're getting new patients all the time, so you'll have company soon enough."

I swallowed. This great big dormitory all to myself. It was something I had dreamt about sometimes at home on Sjömansgatan when it was difficult to find space to sit among my rabble of siblings. I thought how happy I would be to have them here now. There would be plenty of space for all of us. Mama too.

I walked slowly over to the window at the far end of the dormitory. We were high up. Tree tops stretched as far as the eye could see, and I caught a glimpse of the lake we had driven past.

"I'll take this one, thank you," I said, laying my hand on the cold, white-painted headboard of the bed closest to the window on the right.

"That would have been my choice too," Sister Petronella said with a smile. "Shall we start unpacking?"

She put my travel bag on the bed, opened it and started haphazardly pulling out my things. I only just managed to dive forward and grab *Robinson Crusoe* before it hit the floor.

Next to the bed was a small chest of drawers. I put my book, spinning top, litho prints and photograph in the top drawer while Sister Petronella hung my clothes in a narrow cupboard. My doll Rosa got to sit on top of the chest of drawers. I thought she looked more surprised than usual.

I'm too big for dolls really, but it was nice having Rosa with me. Besides, her red-chequered dress added a splash of colour to all the whiteness.

"Right then," said Sister Petronella. "Now I think it's time for Miss Stina to rest awhile before supper. There's a chamber pot under the bed and drinking water in the jug by the door. Don't go wandering off, just stay here in the ward. See the little cord here on the wall?"

I did. A rather thick white cord with a round bead on the end.

"If you pull on it a bell will ring down in the ward sister's room. But only if it's really necessary. No mischief."

I shook my head. I would be very careful not to pull the cord. I pictured a huge bell ringing loudly right next to stern old Sister Emerentia and her rushing furiously down the corridor. That didn't seem like a good idea.

"All right then! Time to get some rest now," Sister Petronella said and disappeared through the door.

I heard her footsteps disappear down the corridor. Then all was quiet. Very, very quiet. I had never heard such silence before.

I had another coughing fit and my coughs echoed like gunshots around the large empty room. So quiet. So white. How strange everything was. I don't really know what I had imagined, but I probably would have guessed there would be more colours and sounds in the sanatorium. And other children too.

I sat on the edge of my bed and sniffed my cardigan. Mama. I wondered what they were doing at home. Were they thinking of me? Were they worried? I would write them a letter as soon as I could. Sister Petronella would surely give me a pen and paper.

What would I write? *I have come to a castle deep in the forest.* They would probably think I was making it up, even though it was more or less true.

I didn't feel like resting. I went over to the window again instead. The window sill was wide and sturdy, it would be a good spot for sitting if I could get up there. I tried to pull myself up, but my chest tightened and I had to give in. I looked out from where I stood on the floor.

How beautiful it was outside. Autumn had come and yellowing birches peeked out here and there from among the pines. I saw some people moving around on the ground outside, much to my delight—the solitude was starting to feel almost creepy. Some were nurses, I could tell from their white clothes. The others must be patients like me. But they looked very old. Some moved with sticks, others sat on benches.

Then I noticed two other buildings down by the lake. They looked more like houses than hospital buildings. Big, beautiful houses made of dark wood. Who lived there? Sister Emerentia perhaps?

When I turned to look in the other direction and pressed my cheek right up against the glass, I spied another building. It was made of grey stone, just like the sanatorium, but this one had a pointed roof with a cross at the top. A church! How interesting. I could write about it in my letter home to Mama and the others. *The sanatorium is so big that it even has its own church*, I would write.

# 3

# Evening Wash

It's very difficult to rest when someone tells you to. But I tried.

I took off my boots and lay down on the bed. It was very firm and the sheets were rough like newspaper. I shut my eyes and tried to think of anything other than my family back home.

Sometimes, when I get bored, I like to cook up romantic stories for myself, stories I would never dare write down. If someone else read them I might die of embarrassment there and then!

Once I saw a painting in an art dealer's shop window. It showed a knight and a maiden standing with their faces very close together, just about to kiss. He was tall and strong and had shoulder-length brown hair.

The maiden's curly golden hair reached all the way down to her waist, and she had her face tilted upward and her eyes closed as the knight was leaning over her. Looking at it made me feel tingly all over. It was hanging in that window for several weeks, and I came up with all sorts of excuses to walk past it. I preferred to go alone, because Olle or Edith would only get annoyed at me if I insisted on stopping to stare at some painting. This was before I got sick, of course.

And then one day it was gone, replaced with a dull painting of flowers in a vase. I supposed some rich man had bought the knight and maiden to hang up in his house. I was glad that I had gone to look at the painting so many times while I could, because the knight and maiden became sort of etched into my memory. Any time I needed to make up a romantic story, all I had to do was bring them to mind and let my imagination wander.

I must have fallen asleep at last because I was jolted awake when the door flew open and Sister Emerentia marched in with two other nurses in tow. One was pushing a small trolley and the other was carrying folded white cloths. Sister Petronella wasn't there, and these two nurses seemed at least as frightened of Sister Emerentia as I was.

"Get up," she ordered.

Dutifully, I struggled out of bed.

"Get undressed, it's time for your evening wash."

It was awful. I moved slowly, fumbling with the buttons on my cardigan because Sister Emerentia was glaring at me with such an angry expression. I finally succeeded and stood by my bed in nothing but my underwear.

Not all the children on our block back home have both bodices and bloomers, but my sisters and I do. Clean too, Mama makes sure of it. But there was no hiding the fact that my underwear was patched and mended here and there. They had already seen plenty of use when Edith inherited them, and were even more tattered by the time they became mine. I wondered if they might be more seams than fabric by the time they were passed down to Ellen. I felt ashamed standing there like that. I hadn't been prepared for it at all.

The two nurses came closer and started scrubbing my arms and legs with damp rags. They were rough and made my skin go all red.

"Lice?" said Sister Emerentia, making the word sound like a whiplash.

One nurse inspected my hair and shook her head.

I was offended. Yes, I come from a poor household, but I have the sort of mother who gets the lice comb out every week if necessary. So often, in fact, that eventually Olle just cut off all his hair, which Lars and Erik promptly wanted to copy, so all three of them became practically bald.

Then they wanted me to take off my underwear as well and put on clean clothes. It felt strange getting stark naked in front of three women I had never met before. I had been naked at the bathhouse, but that felt normal because everyone else was naked too. I supposed this was just the way things were done in sanatoriums.

In any case, I didn't have to stand there naked for more than a few seconds before I was given a stiff cotton nightshirt to put on, which was just as coarse as the bedsheets. And that was the evening wash over with.

Outside, darkness was falling. One of the nurses rolled the trolley forward and lifted a lid to reveal a bowl of porridge, two large pieces of bread with butter and anchovies, and a glass of milk. It was only then that I realized how hungry I was. I hadn't seen this much food since last Christmas when we got a food parcel from the church!

"Am I to eat here in the dormitory?" I asked gingerly.

"Yes, what else did you expect?" Sister Emerentia scoffed. "A window table at the Bourse Gentleman's Club?"

Well, no. But I *had* hoped I'd be allowed out of that room, at least for a little while. I didn't say anything though, I just sat down and started eating straight from the little trolley. The porridge was hot and filling, and the milk was creamy and sweet.

"Tomorrow you'll meet Dr Hagman," said Sister Emerentia. "You will answer his questions directly, no mischief."

Why did everyone seem so convinced that I was going to get up to mischief? I've always been a good, thoughtful girl. Besides, these days I'm too weak to get up to anything, even if I wanted to.

"Yes, Sister Emerentia," I said in as clear a voice as I could manage. I didn't want her to know how much she scared me. This is always my way with people that make me nervous. I make a show of being sure and confident, but only on the outside.

"Right, eat up your porridge now, then it's time for bed. Sister Ingeborg will fetch the dishes later."

"Yes, Sister Emerentia," I said in perfect unison

with the nurse she had called Sister Ingeborg. It sounded so funny that I wanted to laugh—but didn't dare.

Bless you, Olle, for giving me *Robinson Crusoe*. I don't know what I would have done without it on my first night at Raspberry Hill. After Sister Ingeborg had wheeled away the trolley with the empty bowl and wished me good night, I was supposed to rest again. But I couldn't get to sleep after napping in the car and before supper. Consumptive or not, there is a limit to how much rest I need.

At least I had Robinson Crusoe for company. I curled up in the cardigan Mama knit for me and read several chapters before the room grew too dark to see the text. There was an electric lamp by my bed but I didn't know if I was allowed to turn it on.

I put down the book and gazed at the sky outside my window instead. It was a starry autumn evening. The moon was pushing up from behind the pine trees. And it was quiet again, so quiet.

I felt strange inside. Wrong somehow. It didn't feel like I belonged in the sanatorium. There I was among all the whiteness in my thirty-coloured cardigan, disturbing the silence with my cough. I had barely had a chance to breathe that fresh air everyone had been going on about either. But it wasn't long before sleepiness caught up with me.

# 4

# Ruben

I was woken up again, this time by a giggle. A soft little chuckle that I probably wouldn't have even noticed back home in the city. But it cut through the silence of Raspberry Hill and pulled me out of a strange dream in which Sister Petronella was sitting behind the wheel of a red motor car.

The giggling came from a little boy. He was sitting perched on the window sill that I had tried to climb up before. He was younger than me, maybe seven or eight years old. He had a mop of fair hair that stuck out in all directions and was wearing a similar nightshirt to mine and thick rag socks.

Seeing him made me both happy and cross. Happy that there was at least one other child at Raspberry Hill. Cross because he was sitting there in the moonlight reading my *Robinson Crusoe*!

He looked at me and grinned.

"What a silly name, Friday," he said.

I didn't know what to say. Not that I needed to say anything—the boy just carried on.

"Would months sound as silly? Hello, my name is Dr September Hagman. Or times of day! Nice to meet you, the name's Quarter-Past-Seven."

He laughed heartily. I didn't find it all that funny, but felt the corners of my lips draw upwards nonetheless.

"Careful with my book, my brother gave it to me," I said.

"What a kind brother! Do you have lots of brothers and sisters?"

"Five."

"I win! I've got twelve!"

"You do not!"

"I do too!"

"What are their names?"

The boy went quiet for a moment. I had him now. I couldn't be fooled so easily. But he was just taking a breath to prepare.

"Enok Peter Emmelie Maja Ruben Stig Olof Greta Beata Tom Albert Margit and little Elisabeth," he said without the slightest pause.

"Say them again," I said, still not convinced.

"Enok Peter Emmelie Maja Ruben Stig Olof Greta Beata Tom Albert Margit and little Elisabeth," he said, just as quickly and certainly.

I counted quickly on my fingers as he reeled off the names.

"Ha, you're lying! That was thirteen names and you said you only had twelve siblings."

"Yes, but Ruben is me," he said and laughed again so hard that his whole body shook.

I had to admit defeat. He must really have twelve siblings. Stranger things have happened.

"What's your name?"

"Stina."

"What do you think of Raspberry Hill, Stina?"

"I'm not sure yet. It's very big. Which ward are you in?"

"Ward Twenty-three. It's quite far away."

"Do they know you're up and about? They told me I had to stay in this room."

"Sure, they always say that."

"Have you been here long?"

"A while. Long enough to know which nurses are lazy about the night rounds. Tonight it's Ingeborg. Or Scaredy-Mouse, as I call her."

It was very cruel, but I couldn't help but laugh. Sister Ingeborg did look like a scared little mouse.

"Is Sca— I mean, is Sister Ingeborg lazy about the rounds?"

"Oh no. She is always on time. She'll come by in about ten minutes so don't be startled when she peeks in. When Missy is on nights you're free to do what you want."

"Who's Missy?"

"Sister Petronella, of course! She usually just falls asleep or sits chatting with the ambulance drivers. Then you can walk around wherever you want and never get caught. Good, huh?"

I listened carefully to everything Ruben was saying. He might have been making it all up, but if he wasn't, then he was the first person I had met at Raspberry Hill who had actually taken the time to explain things to me.

He hopped down from the window sill so lightly that his feet didn't make a sound when they hit the floor, then he put the book back on my chest of drawers and his expression grew a little more serious.

"It's a very nice book. I understand why you want to be careful with it. Sorry for borrowing it without asking."

"Oh, that's all right."

"Maybe I could come back and read a bit more some time?"

"Yes, you're very welcome!"

I truly meant it. It wouldn't feel as lonely at Raspberry Hill if I had a friend. Even if he was all the way in Ward Twenty-three.

Ruben slipped away as quietly as a shadow and, sure enough, a few minutes later I heard the door open again. I pretended to be asleep but between my eyelashes I glimpsed Sister Ingeborg peeking behind the curtain, just like Ruben had said she would.

# 5

# Dr Hagman

I didn't sleep very well. Then again, I never do these days. My cough kept waking me up. At least I didn't get blood on the sheets. That would have been embarrassing, to stain such perfectly clean sheets.

In the morning Sister Petronella came in with porridge. I was happy to see her again, she seemed kinder and more cheerful than the other nurses. Ruben had called her Missy, maybe because she was so young and pretty.

"Now eat up and get yourself dressed. Dr Hagman is waiting."

It occurred to me that whenever a nurse came into the room everything suddenly became very urgent.

Eat your food, change your clothes, plait your hair. Whereas in between their visits there was nothing to do at all. It all seemed rather off-balance to me, but of course I obliged and went as fast as I could.

Sister Petronella had brought me some clothes. A brown striped dress with a white apron. They weren't new but they were much nicer than anything I had brought in my travel bag. The dress was a little too big but I felt very smart in it. Like a respectable, presentable young lady. Almost good enough for a graduation party.

"Come on now, off we go."

Sister Petronella and I walked out into the long corridor once again. Suddenly I felt a little nervous. What if Dr Hagman was as strict as Sister Emerentia? I didn't dare ask Sister Petronella, I should have asked Ruben when I had the chance. He would definitely know.

"Come on, pick up your feet! Hurry, hurry! The chief doctor can't wait for ever!"

So Hagman was the *chief* doctor. He would be just as scary as the chief nurse, I had no doubt.

We went downstairs. Along another corridor. Right turn. Another staircase, a narrower white one made of iron. Down we went. A few nurses scurried past.

It struck me that I would never find my way back to my ward alone. Eventually we arrived.

An older lady in a grey dress was sitting behind a desk. She stood up when she saw us, went over to a door and reached for the handle.

"You may go in. Georg is expecting you."

"Thank you, Mrs Hagman," said Sister Petronella.

Mrs Hagman smiled at me but there was something about her smile that made me even more worried. Her mouth was friendly but her eyes were stern. I supposed she must be the chief doctor's wife.

My heart was beating like a drum as I went into Dr Hagman's office. I was so amazed by what I saw that I actually stopped in the doorway, staring like a fool, and Sister Petronella had to give me a nudge.

It was the most opulent room I had ever seen! Bookshelves from floor to ceiling, thousands of books with embellished gold spines. A crystal chandelier hung from the ceiling and there was a huge *Arabian Nights* rug on the glossy parquet floor. By the window was a large desk made of dark wood, facing a suite of dark green velvet sofas. I barely dared breathe, everything in the room looked so expensive and fragile.

"Well, hello there," said a voice.

Oh how delighted I was! The man behind the large desk didn't look stern at all. He looked more like a kindly grandfather with his white beard and bushy side-whiskers. He looked at me curiously over the rim of his small glasses. Then he got up from his black chair and came over to me.

"Little Stina, I presume? Who has come all the way to Raspberry Hill to help us with our research!" he said.

His voice was loud and deep but it sounded like there was a little laughter always there in the background.

I curtsied.

"Do sit down," said Dr Hagman. "We can have a little chat before Sister Emerentia comes."

Oh no, was she coming too? I had hoped it would just be the doctor, Sister Petronella and me.

"Tell me now, Stina, how have you found Raspberry Hill so far?"

I thought for a moment.

"Big. And rather dreary."

I hoped the doctor wouldn't be upset that I found his beautiful sanatorium dreary.

"And very modern," I hastened to add.

Dr Hagman laughed.

"Yes, I realize our sanatorium must seem like a veritable haunted castle for a little girl like you, Stina. But more staff and more patients are coming soon. And it certainly is modern, you're right about that."

There was a knock at the door but it wasn't Sister Emerentia. It was a man. He was younger than Dr Hagman, maybe the same age as Mama. He was also wearing a white coat.

"Excuse me, Dr Hagman," he said when he saw me. "I didn't know you were with a patient."

"Not just any patient, I might add," said Dr Hagman, "but Miss Stina, one of the most important people in our tuberculosis research. Stina, may I present my colleague, Dr Funck."

I was unsure what to do. I was sitting down. Was I supposed to stand up to curtsy? Or was a nod enough? What was proper etiquette in such a grand room with such refined people?

"Good day," I said, much too quietly.

"Good morning, miss," said Dr Funck, disinterested. "Dr Hagman, I'm doing the rounds in Wards One to Twelve now. Could I possibly borrow Sister Petronella?"

I noticed Sister Petronella blush and look rather pleased. Dr Hagman waved his hand.

"Of course, off you go, Sister."

Then Dr Hagman and I were left alone. My nerves had calmed down because the doctor seemed kind. But I still felt completely out of place in this elegant room. The chair I was sitting on was very fancy and rather uncomfortable. There was something hard inside the seat that rubbed against my bony back, and the velvet itched. My feet didn't reach the floor.

"Tell me, Stina, my little friend. Has anyone explained to you why you are here?"

I nodded.

"Very good. As you know, lung disease is the scourge of our time. And the most vulnerable are young children in the inner cities, just like you. It is my conviction that with the right medication and a salubrious environment, we can bring about improvements in the majority of patients."

That was a lot of long words in one sentence but I nodded again.

"Alas, sanatorium stays and medicine cost money, as I'm sure you understand. Money that not everyone has. My hope is to establish a fund to finance care for the most vulnerable. But to attract financiers to such a humanitarian effort, I need proof that my methods do indeed have the desired effect. And this is where Miss Stina comes into the picture. Do you understand, little friend?"

I'd lost the thread a while ago, but I gave it a shot.

"I'm to be given medicine and fresh air and if I get healthier, maybe rich people will want to give money so that other poor children can have the same as me," I said tentatively.

Dr Hagman laughed again.

"What an excellent summary! Significantly more succinct than mine! How about a glass of fruit squash?"

I wasn't going to say no to that. The doctor poured a large glass of blackcurrant squash from a carafe and handed it to me. It was delicious.

"But I want to be very clear on one point," Dr Hagman continued. "Tuberculosis is a truly terrible disease. You will receive the best possible care, but unfortunately there is no guarantee that the disease will go away."

He looked very sad as he said this.

"I understand that, Dr Hagman," I said quickly. "I understand that I will probably die soon. But if you think I can be of use here at Raspberry Hill, I would like to help. With the research, I mean."

I tried to smile as widely as I could and took another sip of the tasty squash. Dr Hagman looked at me. He appeared thoughtful.

"One thing's for certain. You are a most unusual child. It's not every day one meets a child so astute. Truly exceptional..."

There was another knock at the door and in came Sister Emerentia. She looked at me disapprovingly, but I had come to expect as much. I would probably have found it unnerving if she had given me a sunny smile and a pat on the head.

Dr Hagman and Sister Emerentia examined me for what felt like an eternity. They listened to my lungs and my heart, looked into my ears and my throat. They felt my throat and told me to cough. I had to answer a lot of difficult questions while Sister Emerentia took notes. The worst was when they pricked my arm with a needle to test my blood. I'm so bony that needles scare the life out of me. Not like Olle back home, who sometimes deliberately sticks pins into his hand to prove how brave he is.

I tried my best and the doctor seemed happy with how things went. Finally, their examination was over.

"There now, Stina, with your consent we would like to start your medication with your next meal."

"Yes please," I said politely.

"And now I think it's high time you went for a stroll to get some fresh air. We'll send up a nurse to fetch you some warm clothes. It's a beautiful autumn day out there, but chilly."

Yes, fresh air. Finally they were giving me the chance to get some.

"Thank you very much, Dr Hagman," I said and curtsied.

Mama would have been proud of me. I had behaved like a very well brought-up girl, if I do say so myself.

# 6

# The Witch

All this talk of fresh air had meant very little to me before, but stepping out onto the front steps of the sanatorium and taking my first deep breath, I started to understand.

The forest air was completely different from the air back on Sjömansgatan. Clean, cold, fresh, and it didn't smell of anything. At home you could always smell something. Herring, smoke, food, an outhouse. I took another deep breath—too deep, and it made me cough for a long time.

I wasn't alone. To my right was a long porch with eight ladies lying in a row on sun loungers made of cane or something. They were wrapped in thick blankets and looked deeply content as they closed their eyes to the autumn sun. Some were wearing elegant hats, I noticed.

A few other patients were walking around the gardens in front of the sanatorium, some arm in arm with a nurse. I looked for Ruben, but he was nowhere to be seen.

Sister Emerentia had told me that I was free to roam the grounds between the sanatorium and the lake but to stay away from the other buildings. Still, I saw no reason why I couldn't explore in that direction a little bit. Just to have a look.

Off I traipsed, greeting anyone who came near me with a shy little nod and hoping that no one would start talking to me and asking questions. I had already done so much talking with Dr Hagman; I was spent.

My legs weren't used to walking as much as they had been through the corridors of Raspberry Hill, but it seemed that all the rest and good food I had been given since I got here had made me stronger. It even crossed my mind to run, but I decided against it.

Down by the lake was a beautiful pavilion I hadn't noticed before, with white pillars and a green, dome-shaped roof. I walked to the water's edge just beyond the pavilion and gently touched the water with the tip of my shoe. People must swim here in the summer. But patients with sick lungs like me probably shouldn't go swimming in cold lakes.

I turned around and took a good look at the sanatorium.

In this sunshine, the grey building looked almost beautiful. I tried to figure out which of the second-floor windows was mine, but it was hard to tell. I should have put something in my window to make it easier. I would make sure I remembered to do so next time.

From my spot by the lake I could see the other buildings as well. Two large houses with blackish walls, a steep-pitched red roof and white window frames. I walked slowly along the lake shore to get a better look. The house nearest me was the larger of the two, with a neat sign hanging from the fence.

*Hagman*, it read.

I should have known. Only posh people lived in houses like these. And the chief doctor must be the poshest person in the whole sanatorium. Maybe Dr Funck lived in the other house? That one was further away and Sister Emerentia would probably think I'd gone too close to the houses already.

I felt more energetic than I had in a long time. I had been walking around and standing up for a good few minutes already. Usually I needed to rest and sit down a lot. Over the summer I had barely got out of bed at all.

I could keep going for a little longer at least. I might as well take a look at the church. From a distance, of course.

The steps up from the lake were steep, but I managed to climb them at a steady pace. I only had to stop to cough once.

The church was in a small grove of trees, surrounded by a stone wall that I could just about see over. Gravestones were dotted all over the ground with inscriptions and iron or wooden crosses on top.

Of course. Not everyone gets better, even in sanatoriums. Here lay the unlucky ones.

I wondered what would happen to me if I died at Raspberry Hill. Would I be buried here or at home in the city? Were these graves expensive, I wondered? They must be. We didn't have to bury Papa because he never returned from Tampere. Grandma Josefa was buried at the new cemetery not far from Sjömansgatan. Would I be buried in the same place as Grandma? It would certainly be cheaper than here. Besides, I'm only small. I would take up hardly any space.

I hoped they wouldn't bury me here. It was beautiful at Raspberry Hill, but Mama and my siblings were so far away. Not that it matters when you're dead, of course. But still, it wouldn't feel right.

My head was swimming with thoughts of burials and graves, when suddenly I noticed I wasn't alone at the stone wall. Someone was standing not far away, looking straight at me. It was an old woman. There was something frightening about her even though she was small, barely taller than me. It must have been her eyes, so pale blue that they looked almost white. Her hair was white too, sticking out in wisps from under a thick knitted hood. She looked just like a witch in a fairy tale.

"Rich girl or poor girl?" she asked in a hoarse, raspy voice.

I didn't make a sound. The old woman looked impatient.

"We-ell? Which are you? A rich girl or a poor girl?"

"A poor girl," I mumbled.

The old woman shut her eyes and shook her head. Then suddenly she took a few steps towards me, frighteningly fast. My impulse was to run but it felt as if my boots were pinned to the grass.

"As soon as you get the chance, run away from here," the old woman hissed, her eyes open wide. "Poor children don't fare well here. Just ask them." And she nodded meaningfully towards the church and graves. Then she turned on her heel and waddled off down to the lake.

A terrible coughing fit came over me. I coughed and coughed and had to lean against the wall to keep myself from falling.

Suddenly Sister Petronella appeared by my side.

"Oh, you poor little thing," she said. "You've been out far too long and the cold has got to you! Let's get you inside in the warm, it's soon time for supper."

She put her arm around my waist—I could tell that she was very strong—and started leading me towards the sanatorium. I turned my head to look for the old woman with the white eyes, but she was gone.

That night I lay in bed listening out for Ruben. I had so many questions I wanted to ask him. What did he think of Dr Hagman and Dr Funck? Had he met the witch with the white eyes? Did he know what she meant about rich children and poor children?

When I could no longer hold off sleep, I got up to put *Robinson Crusoe* on the window sill, so Ruben would know he was allowed to read it. I propped my doll Rosa up against the window too, so that next time I went outside I could see her and know which window was mine.

I fell asleep straight away and had horrible dreams. But they faded the moment I woke up. Only the feeling of terror remained because my heart was pounding so hard. The book was still where I had left it.

In the morning Sister Ingeborg came in with a bowl of porridge, soon followed by another nurse carrying a large branch of pine, with needles and cones and everything. She placed it at the foot of my bed.

"What... what is that?" I asked, surprised.

"One of Dr Hagman's methods," said Sister Ingeborg. "Patients who are too weak for woodland walks get a little bit of forest inside instead. It'll do you good."

Clearly I wasn't going to be allowed out after getting such a chill the day before. I was disappointed but also relieved to be able to avoid that scary old woman with the white eyes.

They had started me on my medication. Morning, noon and night I was given a spoonful of a disgusting liquid. It tasted a bit like sugar syrup, which is usually nice, but this was much more bitter. If it weren't for Sister Emerentia holding the spoon, I probably would have retched. I didn't know if I could get used to it. My first dose the previous day had burned like fire in my throat, as it was supposed to, according to Sister Emerentia. My second dose that morning didn't burn quite as much. But goodness me, it was horrid!

They did the rounds just before noon. Dr Hagman, Dr Funck, Sister Emerentia and two sisters I had never seen before walked in. My huge dorm room, usually so empty, was suddenly filled with people.

"So how is my little friend Stina today?" Dr Hagman asked kindly.

"Fine, thank you," I replied.

"I'm afraid I must ask you to be a little more specific. How is your chest feeling?"

I thought about it.

"It hurts."

"More or less than usual?"

"A little less, maybe."

I was examined again, quickly this time.

"We'll continue with her medication according to the plan," Dr Hagman told Sister Emerentia, who was taking notes as usual.

"Well now, little friend. Is there anything else we can do for you?" the doctor asked me.

It struck me that there actually was.

"Well, Dr Hagman, I wonder if I might have a pen and paper? I would very much like to send a letter to my mother and tell her that I have arrived safe and well."

"But of course, little miss! We can arrange that. Just give the letter to one of the nurses when you've finished and we'll add it to my personal outgoing mail. Indeed a valued guest like Miss Stina must be able to write to the people back home."

I think I blushed, though naturally I couldn't see whether or not I had. Dr Hagman always took me so seriously and talked about me as if I were very important and respectable. I wasn't used to being treated this way and could think of nothing intelligent to say back.

After supper I finally wrote my letter.

*Dear Mother, Olle, Edith, Ellen, Lars and Erik,*

*I find myself in a castle in the woods, would you believe it? The sanatorium is so enormous that we have our very own church! Taking care of me are Dr Hagman, Sister Emerentia and Sister Petronella.*

*Everyone has been very kind to me. I have a pine
branch by my bed and I am given medicine that tastes
awful three times a day.*

What else should I write? I really wanted to tell them
about Ruben, but I was almost starting to think he
had been a dream. I'd have liked to write a little
more about how strict Sister Emerentia was too, but
I worried that she might open my letter and read it.
No, better to write something that might cheer up
Mama.

*The air is very fresh here at Raspberry Hill. Yesterday
I walked for a long time without having to stop and
cough.*

And then a witch with white eyes came and ruined
everything, I thought, but I couldn't write that.

*I hope you are all well.
    Best regards, your Stina.
    PS. Olle: Ferte opem misero Stina!*

That last sentence must seem strange if you hav-
en't read *Robinson Crusoe*. But Olle has. He would

understand that it was my way of thanking him for the book.

It was a short letter, but it took me a long time to write it out neatly, so it would have to do.

# 7

# Nocturnal Adventures

I nearly finished reading *Robinson Crusoe* that afternoon. I would have to start it from the beginning again if I wanted to read some more. There didn't seem to be any other children's books at Raspberry Hill, at least not on the shelves in Dr Hagman's office.

Sister Petronella came in with my supper. First she cleaned me up a little and dressed me in a fresh nightshirt. She was yawning widely the whole time.

"How on earth am I going to manage the night shift when I'm so tired already?" she moaned.

A thought struck me. Sister Petronella was working tonight! The one who, according to Ruben, would either fall asleep or hang around with the ambulance drivers. Maybe Ruben would come and visit again tonight!

Ruben came! I don't know exactly what time it was, but at some point in the middle of the night my cough woke me up and I saw him sitting in his same spot on the window sill with a cheeky look on his face.

"Hello," he said happily.

"Hello," I said back. "It's Sister Petronella's night tonight."

"I know! Get dressed and let's go!"

I hadn't expected that. I didn't have the nerve to go anywhere!

"I wouldn't dare," I whispered.

"What? Don't you want to look around? Missy won't notice you're gone and I know every hiding place in the whole building!"

I hesitated. Everyone, with the possible exception of Sister Emerentia, had been very kind to me so far, and I had no desire to anger them by being naughty. On the other hand, I was incredibly curious. And if I didn't go with Ruben he might go off on his own adventure and I wouldn't get to ask him all those questions I had been wondering about.

I plucked up my courage, climbed out of bed and went over to the cupboard where my clothes were hanging up. I put on my long socks and cardigan.

"Carry your boots in your hand," Ruben whispered. "It'll be quieter that way."

"Are we going outside as well?"

"Of course!"

This was outrageous. It was silly and reckless—but exciting.

"Come on!" he whispered.

I opened the door a crack. The corridor outside was almost completely dark, but for the dull glow of a paraffin lamp hanging from the ceiling some distance away. All was quiet in the sanatorium. Ruben slipped past me and moved silently across the floor. I tried to walk quietly behind him but my footsteps made loud thuds compared to his. Sneaking around clearly wasn't a skill of mine.

I assumed we would head for the main staircase, but Ruben beckoned me to follow him in the opposite direction.

"There's another staircase over here," he whispered.

The other staircase was made of wood, and so small and narrow that you could walk past it without even noticing it was there. It was pitch-black and I had to be very careful.

"Sixteen steps, then it turns, then another sixteen steps," I heard Ruben whisper in front of me.

"Where are we going?"

"You'll see."

We had come down to the first floor. The corridor here was exactly the same as the one upstairs, but there was a light shining nearby and I could hear a woman's loud, exaggerated laughter. Ruben grinned, held a finger to his lips and gestured for me to follow. We tiptoed towards the light, crawled behind a large cupboard in the corridor and peeked into the room where the laughter was coming from.

It was Sister Petronella. She was sitting with two men in white and drinking out of a flowery porcelain cup. The men were laughing too but not as loudly. These must be the ambulance drivers Ruben had mentioned.

We crept back along the corridor, Ruben pointed out another staircase and we continued downstairs.

The corridor down on the ground floor looked different. I could tell even in the half-light. It was much fancier, with flowers painted on the walls, and ornate sofas and doors, and plant pots here and there. More homely too. This is what I imagined a hotel must look like.

"Welcome to the madams' ward," whispered Ruben.

"What's that?"

"It's where rich women come and stay because they want to tell their friends that they've been resting in a sanatorium. They're not really sick, they just pay lots of money."

I thought about those ladies in elegant hats lying under blankets out on the porch. They must be the 'madams'.

The doors on this corridor were closer together, which I supposed meant that there were more rooms on the ground floor but they were smaller. Wealthy ladies probably wouldn't want to sleep in a shared dormitory.

I almost fainted with fear when a nurse suddenly came out of a door further down the corridor. If she had turned her head she would have seen me and Ruben even in the darkness. Thankfully she didn't and disappeared through another door instead. That was close.

"Have your shoes ready, we'll slip out through the kitchen door," whispered Ruben and I followed behind him again.

We came down to the kitchen of Raspberry Hill. It must be one of the biggest kitchens in the world, I thought. We padded across the clean-scrubbed, black-and-white-chequered floor, past polished benches and vast pots big enough to make soup for hundreds of people. At the far end was a door that looked out onto the grounds.

"Is it locked?" I whispered.

"Try and see."

I grabbed the handle and pushed. The door opened and we were hit by the cold night air. Time to put my boots on.

"We'll run to those trees over there," said Ruben. "One, two, three—go!"

We ran. When we had arrived safely in the shadow of the two large pines, a realization struck me.

"Ruben! I didn't cough once on the way down! And I even ran!"

"There, you see? Maybe that branch in your room is helping after all."

I felt exhilarated and more alive than I had in a long time. But at the same time, I was a little shaken when I thought about how easily a nurse could have discovered us if I had coughed on the way out. I supposed I could have fibbed and said I'd been sleepwalking and couldn't find my way back to my ward...

"Duck! Someone's coming," Ruben hissed.

I dived behind a bench and held my breath. I could hear footsteps approaching from the direction of the grand houses. Carefully, I peeked between the boards of the bench and saw Dr Hagman walking past. Instead of a white coat he was wearing a regular suit. His pipe glowed in the dark and he was humming a familiar tune. 'The Lullaby Waltz', perhaps. He hadn't seen us, thank goodness.

The chief doctor was walking with a long, purposeful stride, and in just a few seconds he arrived at the front steps and walked up into the sanatorium.

"He lives over there, doesn't he?" I asked, pointing at the big house.

"Yes, with Mrs Hagman."

"Who lives in that other house?"

"Dr Funck and Sister Emerentia. Well, not together, of course. It's split into different apartments."

Ruben seemed to know everything there was to know about Raspberry Hill. All I had to do was ask.

"Ruben, why is there a church here?"

He laughed.

"A church? There's no church here. Do you mean the mortuary?"

"Mortuary?"

"Yes, it's where they take the patients who can't be cured by fresh air and pine trees. Don't you know what a mortuary is?"

It was a good job it was so dark, because I felt very foolish and must have turned bright red. Of course I knew what a mortuary was. I grew up just a few blocks away from the new cemetery and saw dead people in coffins being carried there almost every day, to the brick buildings where they were kept before they were buried. But I had never seen a mortuary that looked just like a church.

Goodness, it was cold. My whole body was trembling, try as I might to wrap my cardigan tightly around me. The grass crackled under my boots. Summer was well and truly over.

"I should probably get back now."

We started slowly back towards the kitchen door. The sanatorium looked spooky at night. Only a few windows were lit up, probably where nurses were on night shift.

"Do you want to see the lift?" asked Ruben.

Of course I did. Luckily the door to the kitchen was

still unlocked (imagine if we had been locked out!), so we took off our shoes and crept across the chequered floor. When we got back up to the madams' ward, we went slowly, a few steps at a time, then stopped, hid, listened out and only continued when we were sure the coast was clear. I felt a bit like Robinson Crusoe sneaking up on the flock of llamas.

I could hear people snoring and snorting from behind closed doors. One might swing open at any moment and a nurse could come out and see us. I was terrified, but thrilled too. Not even Olle could have pulled off staying out of sight on a nocturnal adventure like this. I must be braver than I'd thought.

"Here it is," whispered Ruben so quietly I could hardly hear him.

The lift was nothing like I had imagined. It looked like a huge cage without a floor or ceiling. The walls were yellow-painted iron grates and there were thick cables inside. The actual platform that you stood on must have been at another floor.

"It's so big!"

"Well, it has to be, if they're going to wheel a stretcher in there."

"Have you ever been in the lift?"

"Just once."

"What was it like?"

"Oh I dunno. Nothing special."

I could hear laughter echoing somewhere above us. It was probably Sister Petronella and the ambulance drivers. I had lingered by the lift and noticed that Ruben had already got quite far along the corridor. I followed. I wouldn't be able to find my way back to my room without him, so I thought it best not to lose him.

We climbed back up the narrow wooden staircase and made our way through the more modest corridors, the ones that were painted white and light green with no flowery decorations.

Then we came to my door.

"Good night then," Ruben whispered cheerily and scampered away.

I didn't even get a chance to reply before he disappeared into the darkness. And I was still brimming with all the questions I'd never got the chance to ask him!

# 8

# The Rich Child

I woke up in a good mood. I would probably have to lie in bed all day but after spending so much time out and about the night before I didn't really mind.

Sister Ingeborg looked at me suspiciously when she brought me my morning porridge.

"What are you grinning about?"

"Oh, nothing special. I... I had a funny dream!"

Sister Ingeborg just sniffed in response and looked even more like a mouse than usual.

The day turned out to be just as boring as I had expected. Dr Funck examined me on his rounds. The medicine tasted as disgusting as ever. I finished *Robinson Crusoe*.

I considered writing another letter to Mama, a longer one this time. Then I decided against it. They would think I'd gone daft if I started writing every day.

I played with my doll Rosa for a while instead. She was the sick child and I was the doctor. The sick child had to smell pine branches to get better.

It was raining outside.

Robinson Crusoe is scared of having nothing to do on his desert island. But he is all right really, because he can come and go as he pleases. If he decides to make pots or chase llamas there's no Sister Emerentia to stop him and order him to stay in his shelter and rest. I was worse off, forced to lie in bed from morning to night. Thinking. Only the saddest and most difficult thoughts came to mind when I was lying still.

Dying young has its advantages. For one, there's no need to worry about the future. In all honesty, we, the children of war widows on Sjömansgatan, don't have that many opportunities in life. But one can always dream. All my brothers and sisters have dreams.

Olle wants to be a sailor, I think I've mentioned that already. He dreams of travelling to far-off lands where it's warm all year round, the people have dark skin, and brightly coloured flowers and fruits grow everywhere. I hope he gets to do it one day, but Mama needs him at home for now, so maybe not for a little while.

Edith wants more than anything to bob her hair and draw on thin black eyebrows, just like Clara Bow. She dreams of being a saleswoman in one of the up-market shops that sell gloves, hats or other beautiful things for elegant ladies. And then she'll be courted by a handsome student who will take her out to the patisserie. Not just yet of course—Edith is only thirteen years old. But in two or three years' time.

Even little Lars and Ellen know what they want to be. Lars wants to become a soldier, just like Papa. Ellen wants to ride circus horses or walk the tight rope. Erik wants to be a hurdy-gurdy man, mainly because he wants a real-life monkey of his own. Once we saw a hurdy-gurdy man who had a small monkey with him in the square by Saluhallen. Erik still talks about it. Olle teases him and says the audience would get confused seeing Erik cranking the hurdy-gurdy and the monkey collecting money because they look exactly the same.

"Maybe you can take turns and the monkey can play when your arm starts to ache."

Erik never gets angry, luckily, and instead just laughed and made himself a pretend hurdy-gurdy using a few sticks and a wooden box. No music came out of it, but Erik whistled and the rest of us applauded and tipped him with buttons instead of money when he passed his hat.

Before I got sick I used to do it too: fantasize about what I might be when I grew up. I used to think that if I could learn to write better and faster, I could write romantic stories and funny serials and sell them to magazines. I even came up with a pseudonym. I'd call myself: the Purple Duchess. But those thoughts are a thing of the past. I would rather listen to my siblings talk about their dreams.

How dreadful it would be not to know how my siblings are doing after I'm dead. I hope there will be some way of looking down on them to see if they really do become circus performers and sailors or have to settle for washing, ironing and sewing like Mama. And I am so curious to know whether they will have families of their own when they grow up as well. Maybe a whole gaggle of little children who hear the story of poor Auntie Stina who died so young.

Edith is the only one so far who seems interested in love and that sort of thing. She is desperately in love with a boy named Caj Tengström. He is terribly old, at least eighteen, and barely knows that Edith exists. It's been a long time since I've been in town with Edith, but before I got sick, every time we bumped into Caj Tengström the exact same scene took place: Edith stopped, grabbed my wrist so hard that I almost yelped, and then squealed, "Oh no, Stina! There he is! I think I'm going to faint!"

But she never did faint. Instead, she turned as red as a peony and leapt into the first doorway she found before Caj Tengström could see her. I didn't understand; it all seemed the wrong way round to me. If the plan was for Caj Tengström to become as enamoured of Edith as she was of him, surely it would make more sense to stay where he could see her?

"You're just a silly little kid who doesn't under-stand a thing," Edith sniffled when I tried to say so.

I do know a thing or two—how else would I be able to invent romantic stories about knights and maidens, for example? But as for the idea of me being the heroine in one of those stories... no, that's far too ludicrous.

Love seems complicated. I'm glad it's something I'll never have to deal with.

———

That evening, something actually happened. Finally. Sister Emerentia came into my room and told me to follow her. Naturally, I was terrified. At first I assumed she had found out about our nocturnal gallivanting and that I would surely be beaten, but as it turned out, it was bath time. There was a large washroom near the kitchen on the ground floor, with several sizeable bathtubs in a row. One of them was filled with steaming hot water.

"Go on, in you get. Stop being a baby," Sister Emerentia said sternly.

I gritted my teeth and sat there feeling like I was going to be boiled like a potato, but then I got used to the heat and it became very pleasant actually. I was just about to close my eyes to relax and enjoy myself when Sister Ingeborg started scrubbing me. Fancy being scrubbed so hard every other night! Then again I supposed there weren't many other patients for the nurses to take care of, so they had to make do with me.

Afterwards, Sister Ingeborg braided my hair. She pulled and tugged and complained. I do have very unruly hair. It won't comb into straight sections. No matter how you try, it curves so that one braid comes out thicker than the other. Mama doesn't even try, she thinks uneven braids will do just fine. But Ingeborg was stubborn and struggled with it so much that I wondered whether I would have any hair left to braid when she was done.

On the way out of the washroom, I caught sight of my reflection in a mirror. How funny I looked! All red and puffy from the heat with two braids that were so tight they stuck straight out behind my ears. But my cheeks had become a little rounder. After all, I was eating my fill several times a day. Porridge, soup, cabbage rolls, bread and gruel appeared so often that I barely had time to get hungry between meals.

I felt very guilty. Back home they all have to share small bowls of thin broth. And here I was slurping hearty soup containing big chunks of meat. How unfair it was.

Indeed, a trolley with a bowl of porridge on it was waiting for me when I got back to my dorm. My medicine was ready too; Sister Ingeborg poured a spoonful and I dutifully opened wide. It didn't taste quite as awful as before, I thought. Sickly and gooey but not quite as bitter. I could get used to it.

Before I fell asleep, I tried to think about the knight and maiden for a little bit. But they didn't want to appear in my head. I don't know why. Instead, all I could think of was Sister Petronella and Dr Funck, so I made up a romantic story about them. It became very naughty, but Sister Petronella probably would have liked it.

Ruben didn't come to me that night, but we couldn't have gone out anyway because it was pouring with rain. I woke up coughing several times, and each time I hoped I would see him sitting on the window sill. But there was no one there.

Over the next few days I became frightfully bored. I was only allowed outside a few times. When I did go out I noticed that there were many more ladies under blankets out on the porch, at least fourteen. There were several patients shuffling around the garden as well, but not a single child.

I understood now why some of the patients moved so laboriously out in the garden. They had tuberculosis, like me, and Dr Funck had tried to cure them by injecting gas into their lungs with a large needle. It sounded really horrible, but luckily it seemed to be only for grown-ups. The method had helped several people in Germany, apparently. Well, that's what I overheard from other patients anyway.

One day I was sitting on the steps when an elegant motor car drove up and Dr Funck came outside to greet a woman called Mrs Bergendahl. She was very chic, dressed in a hat, fur stole and cream-coloured autumn coat.

"Thank goodness I'm here, Dr Funck," said Mrs Bergendahl. "The city air has really taken its toll on me this year, I am utterly wretched."

Hardly, I thought. Mrs Bergendahl looked perfectly healthy. Like a rich lady who goes to the patisserie three or four times a week. But if she wanted to pay lots of money to lie under a blanket and breathe in the forest air, what did I care?

Then suddenly along came another car. When it stopped I was most surprised to see a little girl inside. She must have been about the same age as me, but otherwise we couldn't have been more different. She looked like one of those expensive dolls in the K.F. Winters toy shop. Long curly hair, tied at the back with a black silk bow. Red coat, shiny black shoes, white blouse. But she was very thin and pale. A man and a woman had to more or less lift her out of the car. I supposed they must be her parents. I was so curious that I completely forgot how rude it is to stare. It felt like a long time since I had seen another child, except Ruben of course. No other children had moved into my ward so far. Maybe this girl would? I tried to smile at her but she seemed to look straight through me.

Then Sister Ingeborg came out onto the steps.

"Good afternoon, Dr Hagman is expecting you."

The family went into the sanatorium and I was left standing on the front steps. I started thinking about the scary old woman who had asked if I was rich or poor. There would be no need to ask this little girl, you could tell from a mile off that she was rich.

She would probably do better than me then, if what the old woman had yelled was true, that poor children don't fare well at Raspberry Hill. Though I had never fared better, what with my smart, clean clothes and all the food I could eat.

I decided to put the witch's words out of mind. She probably just wanted to scare me. Who knows why.

All evening I lay in bed hoping the little girl would be brought up to Ward Fourteen, but she wasn't. Maybe she had gone back home again. Or been put in Ward Twenty-three with Ruben.

The thought of this irritated me immensely.

# 9

# Kristin

Ruben hadn't visited in a few nights. I was starting to worry. I didn't even know how seriously sick he was. He had seemed healthy and full of beans the last time I saw him, but you never knew. What if he had taken a sudden turn and was too weak to walk around?

I wondered how far it was to Ward Twenty-three. Did I dare go looking for it myself one night? Just to make sure he was all right. And to remind him that I existed. Maybe that new rich girl was taking up all of his attention...

I'd also started losing track of how long I'd been at Raspberry Hill. It would have been wise to do what Robinson Crusoe does and carve a line into a tree every morning to keep count. But I wasn't allowed to go outside to see the trees every day and I don't think Sister Emerentia would have taken too kindly to notches in my headboard or chest of drawers... All I knew was that the evenings were drawing in and it was still dark outside when the nurses woke me up in the morning with the gruel trolley.

I was on my third reading of *Robinson Crusoe* when the door opened one morning and an older girl came thundering in carrying a mop and bucket. She jolted to a standstill when she saw me, screamed and dropped the bucket, spilling dirty grey water all over the floor.

"Good God in heaven, you gave me a start," she shrieked.

"Sorry," I said, though I was confident I had no reason to be sorry. It's not as if I had jumped out at her and shouted, I had just been lying there reading.

"I'm only s'posed to mop the floor up here, no one said there'd be patients in the dorms," the girl whined.

She looked forlornly at the water that had run almost halfway towards the window.

"Dear Lord, if Sister Emerentia finds out about this..." she moaned.

I climbed out of bed and helped her dry it up. It took a long time. We used a rag each and wrung them out in the bucket after every swab.

"Are you scared of Sister Emerentia?" I asked cautiously.

"Everyone's scared of Sister Emerentia! Even Dr Hagman. Oh sure, he's the chief doctor, but she's the one who makes the decisions around here."

The girl seemed to cheer up once we had cleaned up the spilt water.

"What's your name anyway?" she asked.

"Stina."

"I'm Kristin! Where are you from?"

"Helsinki."

"Ah!" Kristin said with a dreamy look on her face. "Never been to Helsinki. Is it beautiful?"

I thought for a moment. Sjömansgatan wasn't all that beautiful, but the Esplanade Park and all the buildings around Senate Square were spectacular, of course. I'd never really thought about it.

"Yes, quite beautiful."

"I'm sure it is. I live not far from here, on Bruksbacka. It's a farm. Papa cares for the horses and Mama works the dairy. It's a big farm. But I want to be a nurse. I just need to get accepted into the institute first, which is no easy task, believe you me. Are you good at reading?"

"Not bad."

This was something I was actually quite proud of. I had been too sick to go to school for a long time, so instead I'd read anything and everything I could get my hands on while I was lying in bed in the kitchen. My siblings brought home all the newspapers and pamphlets they came across, and our schoolmaster Mr Fransson sometimes lent me his own personal books. Which was very kind of him. So at least I had managed to become a good reader during that summer when I could do nothing but lie in bed and cough.

"I wish I was better at reading," Kristin sighed. "You have to know how to read to be a nurse. All I know is cleaning floors, and I can't even do that right—you saw for yourself. So tell me, is it Dr Funck who takes care of you?"

"Mainly Dr Hagman."

"Pity. Dr Funck is ever so handsome, don't you think?"

"Mm, maybe..."

"I hope more doctors come to work here soon! There were fifteen of them before the fire."

"Did you work here before the fire?"

"Oh yes! But not the night when the fire happened, thank goodness."

"Did the fire spread to the whole sanatorium?"

"No, praise be. Just the East Wing. But the smoke spread all over and they had to close the whole sanatorium to air it out. Ugh, it was horrid, it stank something awful! The East Wing is still out of bounds. Which is just as well, because I wouldn't dare mop a single floor in there."

"Why not?"

Kristin opened her eyes wide and looked both horrified and excited.

"'Cause of *them*, of course. The ones who were trapped in there and couldn't escape the fire."

I swallowed.

"Were... were a lot of people... burnt to death?"

"Not burnt, suffocated by the smoke. Isn't it terrible? They came here to get fresh air and instead they died from poisonous fumes."

"So sad."

I couldn't say why, but it felt like a relief to know that the lives lost were due to smoke, not fire. Of course it made no difference to the people who had died, but I was so very frightened of fire. I couldn't imagine a worse fate. I would rather suffocate. Or at least that's what I thought.

Kristin gave a start.

"Oh, but look at me prattling on when I have plenty more wards to mop! I'd best be getting on!"

It struck me that Kristin probably knew the sanatorium as well as Ruben did. Did I dare ask?...

"Wait, Kristin. Ward Twenty-three. Where is it?"

Kristin, who had started gathering up her mop and rags, paused with a surprised look on her face.

"Ward Twenty-three? Why do you ask?"

"It's not important. I was just wondering if it was far from here?"

"There is no Ward Twenty-three. Not any more. It was one of the wards in the East Wing that was destroyed in the fire. Now I really must be going. Bye, Stina! And thanks for your help!"

Kristin went out into the corridor and disappeared into the next dormitory. I stayed where I was, utterly baffled.

I couldn't get to sleep that night. I felt very ill at ease.

I was sure there must be an explanation. I might have heard Ruben wrong, maybe he hadn't said he was in Ward Twenty-three at all. He might have said three or thirty-three or something completely different. Or there was always a chance he might be teasing me.

Still. Something was making me shiver, even though I was used to the cold by now. Why did I never see Ruben during the day? I wasn't allowed to go out into the grounds every day, but would often look out the window when I was forced to stay inside. I had figured out how to get up onto the windowsill by climbing on a stool, and would sit there for a long time each day, gazing out. I saw other patients, nurses, cars come and go. But never Ruben. And he had seemed at least as healthy as I was, so wouldn't they let him outside at some point too?

Once again, I got the feeling that Ruben might be a dream. But it would be very unusual to have the same dream twice, wouldn't it? Or was I losing my mind?

To distract myself, I wrote a letter home. It turned out to be quite short. I wrote a little about the fire and all the bathtubs in the washroom. Then at the bottom I wrote: *I would very much like to receive a letter back so I know how everyone is doing at home.*

It seemed a little strange that no one had written a single letter to me. On the other hand, I supposed things were going according to plan: that I should come to Raspberry Hill so that Mama and my siblings would get used to not having me at home. Were they forgetting me? It was just as well, then they wouldn't be as sad when I died. But still, a little letter would have made me so happy.

# 10

# The East Wing

The days were melting together more and more at Raspberry Hill. They were all the same. I woke up, ate, rested, got examined, ate, rested, got washed, ate, slept. Sometimes I was allowed to go outside for a bit, sometimes Dr Hagman or Dr Funck decided that I was too poorly and had to stay indoors.

I wasn't getting any better either, quite the opposite. I was coughing even more than before and felt tired most of the time. But I didn't say that in the next letter I wrote home to Sjömansgatan a few days later. Instead I wrote about the lift and the rich ladies lying on the porch taking the air even though they weren't sick.

In any case, I had grown a little braver. I plucked up the courage to walk around the sanatorium during the day, especially when I was allowed to go outside. Really, one of the nurses should have been escorting me down the stairs, but they were lazy and figured I could find my own way. Which I could by now. But I chose to take my time getting there.

I would walk through corridor after corridor, finding secret staircases, taking closer looks at the lift in daylight, and gradually I came to know Raspberry Hill Sanatorium rather well.

I figured out that most of the nurses lived in the West Wing on the floor above the kitchen and washroom. My heart almost stopped one day as I was sneaking through the corridor outside the washroom and suddenly heard a deafening roar. I thought the whole sanatorium was collapsing, but it turned out it was just some of the nurses working a huge mechanical mangle. No wonder the sheets in the sanatorium were pressed so flat. The mangle was the size of a motor car and sounded like a thunderstorm.

If I came across a nurse or patient on my walks around the sanatorium, I just nodded and said hello. No one ever asked me what I was doing or where I was going. Of course, the worst thing would be if

I bumped into Sister Emerentia, but luckily I never had.

One day I came down from the first floor via a staircase I hadn't used before and thought I was lost. But then I realized where I was. Outside Dr Hagman's office. Mrs Hagman wasn't sitting at her desk outside the office, but there was someone else sitting on a bench in the corridor. A child, like me.

No, sadly it wasn't Ruben. It was the rich girl I'd seen get out of the car a few days earlier.

She was so beautiful. She wore a white lace dress with pink bows, and a hat with small flowers on the brim. She noticed me. I should have just got out of there sharpish, but I couldn't resist going over to talk to her. It had been so long since I'd spoken to a girl my own age.

"Hello," I said.

"Hello," mumbled the girl.

Her voice was just as frail and stiff as the rest of her.

"Why are you sitting here?"

"I'm waiting for my parents. Dr Hagman and Mrs Hagman wanted to talk to them alone."

"Why?"

"They won't tell me that either."

"What sort of lung disease do you have?"

"I don't have any lung disease. I have a weak heart."

She said this almost snootily. As if a weak heart were more refined than weak lungs. And maybe it was, how should I know?

"Oh," I said. "My name's Stina, what's yours?"

"Esmeralda."

Then voices could be heard from inside Dr Hagman's office, near the door, as if people were on their way out. I had to hurry. Sister Emerentia might be in there. And I didn't want to disappoint Dr Hagman either, loitering in the corridor without permission.

"I have to go now."

"Goodbye," Esmeralda said quietly.

I had only just turned the corner when I heard the office door open and several grown-up voices echo in the corridor. That was close. I could only hope that Esmeralda wouldn't give me away.

I kept walking as fast as I could without coughing and before I knew it, I was lost. I thought I would emerge into the foyer, but I didn't. And there was me thinking I knew my way around the corridors of the sanatorium. Apparently I didn't at all.

The corridor I had ended up in didn't look the least bit like the others. Well, it had probably been as nice as the madams' ward once, but the paint was flaking off the walls and the floor was dirty. Kristin hadn't been here with her scrubbing brush for a long time, it seemed. I could still make out the flowery borders on the walls, but they were very pale.

A glass wall stood across the corridor. Its door was closed. A sign hung on one of the glass panels.

*Wards* 20–25 *closed until further notice.*

I could feel every hair on my body stand on end. It dawned on me where I was.

I was standing at the entrance to the East Wing.

My first instinct was to turn right back around and find my way back to Dr Hagman's corridor as quickly as possible, but at the same time I was bursting with curiosity. What if I never got this chance again? Why not just look around a little bit?

Slowly, I walked up to the glass wall. The panes were so dirty that I could barely see through them, and I could only just about make out the corridor on the other side. It was even messier in there. I could see some unmade beds, an overturned chair. The walls were covered in soot. There was no doubt about it, this was where the fire had been. This was where all those poor people had lost their lives when the place filled with smoke. It still smelled of soot and smoke, even though it must have been aired out thoroughly since.

I hesitated for a moment before reaching for the door handle. I was almost relieved to find it was locked. I'd been reckless enough already. Going into a closed ward might be dangerous. It was time to turn back now.

Then I heard something terrible! Footsteps approaching! Someone was coming from the same direction I had just come from. There was nowhere to go—I was trapped. How would I explain myself? I had got lost, that much was true, but only after deliberately wandering off without permission.

The steps were coming closer. I looked around wildly.

There was a row of doors to my right, all locked. But the doors were slightly sunk into the walls, leaving a small recess in each doorway. If I pushed myself flat up against one of the doors and whoever was coming didn't look directly at me, I might go unnoticed.

It was my only chance.

I ran into one of the doorways, squashed up into the corner where the door and wall met and took a deep breath.

*Don't cough, don't cough, don't cough.*

Now the footsteps were only a few metres away. The person was walking with a long, purposeful stride. He was humming something too. 'The Lullaby Waltz'.

Dr Hagman walked straight past without looking in my direction, just as I had hoped. He was too busy looking in his jacket pocket, from which he took out a key. At the glass wall, he unlocked the door, went into the East Wing and shut the door behind him. Luckily he didn't turn around, else he would have seen me in my doorway hiding place.

The steps and humming faded into the distance and I finally let out the breath I'd been holding. Then I hurried back the way I had come. I didn't bump into anyone, thank goodness.

I noticed straight away the place I had gone wrong and found the foyer this time. I slipped outside and didn't stop walking until I had got all the way to the grove of trees where Ruben and I had hidden that night.

I sat down on the bench, my whole body shaking. But I wasn't sitting there for long before Sister Petronella appeared on the steps and called to me.

"That's enough fresh air for today," she said cheerily. "Time to come in."

I did as she said. Sister Petronella's smile faded as I came closer.

"What *do* you look like? Your eyes are all red! And what on earth have you been touching? Your whole dress is filthy!"

"Oh... I..." I trailed off.

I'd got my dress dirty pressing myself into that doorway as Dr Hagman passed by.

"It must have been the bench I was sitting on," I lied.

"We'd better hurry so Sister Emerentia doesn't see this," said Sister Petronella. "Or we'll both be in trouble!"

As we walked through the entrance hall I stole a glance at the corridor that led to Dr Hagman's office and on to the East Wing. I might have been mistaken, but I thought I saw Ruben over there, laughing and waving at me. Maybe it was just my imagination, because the next moment, he was gone.

## 11

# Elixir Fifty-seven

That evening I got worse. I was freezing cold and shivered and coughed until I could barely feel my throat. My chest hurt and when the coughs got really bad, drops of blood appeared on my bed sheets.

Oh no.

Just then Sister Ingeborg came in with supper. She let go of the trolley and rushed over to me.

"Dear girl, why didn't you pull the cord?" she cried.

Oh yes, the cord! I had totally forgotten about the cord. But I probably wouldn't have dared pull it anyway. I had seen blood on my sheets before. Did it count as an emergency?

Sister Ingeborg tugged hard on the cord and it wasn't long before the door flew open and Dr Hagman and Sister Emerentia came storming in. And behind them—and I wasn't imagining it, I was seeing clearly despite being mid coughing fit—in came Ruben! He looked as cheerful as ever and walked straight over to the bed opposite mine and sat down with his legs crossed.

Dr Hagman put on his white coat, which had been draped over his arm as he rushed in, and started giving out orders.

"Sister Ingeborg, prepare a hot bath for Stina. Sister Emerentia, I need a bottle of Elixir Fifty-seven, it will stop the bleeding in her throat."

He sat down on the edge of my bed. He looked so kind. I felt guilty, thinking about this caring doctor working to cure my lung disease, and how did I thank him? By snooping around his sanatorium and hiding in doorways when he passed by.

"No need to worry now, little friend. We'll make sure your cough eases up for a while. And then we'll simply have to increase your dose."

Sister Emerentia returned to the room holding a brown glass bottle. I bit my lip—she was looking straight at Ruben! I was sure they would shoo him away with angry voices, but no, Sister Emerentia just ignored him!

Dr Hagman, sitting with his back to Ruben, didn't seem to notice him at all. Then Ruben got up, winked at me, did a little salute to Sister Emerentia (he's got a nerve!) and skipped out the door.

Elixir Fifty-seven was even more disgusting than my usual medicine. It burned my throat terribly when I swallowed it. But then, just a short while later, my throat felt better. I also felt rather dizzy—Elixir Fifty-seven felt like something probably more suited for adults than little children. I had to be pushed out of the room in a wheelchair, and even though I felt very sick, I couldn't help but get excited when I saw where we were going. The lift!

Dr Hagman used a special key and pressed a button. There was a tremendous thumping noise followed by squeaking, and a large cage suddenly rose up to our floor. Dr Hagman opened the door, Sister Emerentia rolled me in, and I got to ride in a lift for the first time in my life. This would be something to write about in my next letter home.

The hot water felt wonderful when Sister Emerentia and Sister Ingeborg lowered me into the bathtub. The whole room was spinning and there was steam everywhere, then I must have blacked out because I don't remember what happened next.

"Jack and Jill on Raspberry Hill..."

Who was singing?

"Jack fell down and broke his crown..."

Why was it so bright? I couldn't see anything at all.

"I have a bad heart," Esmeralda said snobbishly.

She was wearing my cardigan! Oh, that made me cross!

Ruben was sitting on the bed, laughing his socks off. Then he carried on singing at the top of his lungs.

"And Jill came tumbling after..."

"Shoo!" Sister Emerentia shouted and chased him away with a large pine branch.

And there were all the women from our neighbourhood standing in a cluster, looking down at me and clucking their tongues. *Tut-tut-tut.*

"Poor Märta."

"But at the same time it must be a relief!"

"Yes, not to have to worry about the others getting infected, tut."

"It'll be for the best, you mark my words..."

Dr Hagman leaned over me.

"Truly an exceptional child..."

I couldn't breathe.

When I woke up, it was no longer morning. It was already midday! And I wasn't in the bathtub any more either, but in my bed up in Ward Fourteen. Sister Petronella was sitting next to me reading a magazine. When she saw that I was awake she smiled and put the magazine down.

"Good afternoon, Stina! What a fright you gave us yesterday."

"I... how... how long have I been asleep?"

My head throbbed when I tried to sit up. As if someone was bashing me over the skull with a plank of wood.

"No, don't try to get up. You were given strong medicine yesterday. It soothed your throat but your head might smart a little today. You've been asleep for sixteen hours if I'm not mistaken."

Goodness me!

"But you'll get well soon, Stina, you'll see. Dr Hagman is going to take very good care of you. More medicine, more rest. You're going to feel good soon, very good!"

Well, I certainly didn't feel it just then. I felt a bit

like the time I wanted to prove to Olle that I was brave enough to climb up onto the woodshed roof too. I got up fine, but then I lost my balance and fell. My whole back was black and blue that spring. Dr Lundin said it was a miracle I didn't break my neck and legs, and managed to get away with nothing more than bruises and a slight concussion. I felt similarly beat up now.

I heard footsteps out in the corridor and in came Dr Hagman, Dr Funck and Sister Emerentia. Sister Petronella jumped up from her chair.

"Well, look who's woken up," said Dr Hagman cheerfully.

What a strange thing to say. Who else would have woken up? I was the only patient in the whole ward.

I knew the procedure by heart now. The doctor listened to my chest, then my back. I was supposed to take a deep breath and cough gently. Then he counted my heartbeats while looking at his pocket watch, then examined my mouth and ears.

"I shall personally oversee Stina's medication," said Dr Hagman.

He spoke in a much more formal tone when he spoke to his colleagues than when he spoke to me. He sounded almost like a king.

"We shall double her dosage for now."

"Yes, Dr Hagman," said Sister Emerentia.

She looked different today. Stern as usual, but also very tired. And when she looked at me it wasn't with her usual disapproving expression, but sadness. She quickly turned her gaze back down to her notes.

Dr Hagman opened a rectangular briefcase and took out a large brown glass bottle. He poured a big splash into a glass and handed it over to me.

"Here you are, little friend, you might as well take your medicine straight away. Putting it off won't make it taste better."

I drained the glass in one go. It didn't taste all that bad. Syrupy but not too bitter.

"Good girl," Dr Hagman said and gave me a pat on the shoulder.

Sister Petronella sat with me all day. It was nice; she read to me from her magazine. It was a women's magazine so it was mostly about dresses and powders and other things that I didn't find particularly interesting, but Sister Petronella seemed absorbed. At one point, she was in the middle of reading me an article titled 'Things Men Cannot Abide in Young Ladies' and she must have forgotten I was there because she became so engrossed in the text that she stopped reading aloud. In any case, I did hear that you mustn't giggle too much, speak too loudly or use too much perfume. Maybe Edith would be interested to know that.

After my evening meal and medicine, I was left alone again, with orders to pull the cord if I started to feel worse.

I no longer felt dizzy and it was rather pleasant to be alone with my thoughts for a while. I had many and most were about Ruben.

I hadn't had a chance to ask him about Ward Twenty-three yet. And it was strange that he had just walked into my room the day before and escaped without a scolding, even from strict Sister Emerentia.

I thought about Esmeralda too. What was she doing at Raspberry Hill if she had a bad heart, not bad lungs? Raspberry Hill was a sanatorium for lung disease. There were probably a lot of hospitals specifically for heart disease, why didn't she go to one of those? Was she still at Raspberry Hill or had she gone home in that fancy motor car?

And what had Dr Hagman been doing in the East Wing? It must have been very dangerous to go in there, even for the chief doctor.

There was one thing I could do at least. Write home. I was getting worse now, maybe it would be best to prepare them for bad news. So far, I had only written to say that I was doing well. And I never knew which letter might be my last.

But how does one write about such things? *Hello everybody, I'm going to die soon.* No, too blunt. I struggled for a long time before I managed to get down a few lines about what had happened. I included the ride in the lift because I knew that would be of interest to my siblings. Then I sealed the letter, wrote Mama's address on the back and put it in my drawer, right next to *Robinson Crusoe*. Then to sleep.

# 12

# Poisoned

Everyone had seemed so certain that I would get better now that the chief doctor himself was looking after me. But I didn't. I got worse, even though I was being given twice as much medicine. It was a mystery, everyone thought so.

But not me. I had solved the mystery. I solved it about a week after my medication was doubled.

It was during the morning rounds. Dr Hagman was sitting at my bedside with Sister Emerentia standing behind him. The doctor asked her to pass him the bottle of my medicine, and what do you think Sister Emerentia did?

Well, instead of handing him the bottle on the table next to her, she took another identical bottle out of her apron pocket and gave that to him in its place! The doctor didn't notice and I was too dopey to say anything. The medicine tasted so bad it made me grimace.

I didn't have the energy to think about it at the time but gradually I came to understand.

There was only one possible explanation. Sister Emerentia was poisoning me. Or perhaps not directly poisoning me, but she was swapping my medicine for something else that wasn't making me the slightest bit better!

This was why I was getting worse and worse. Sister Emerentia had hated me from the moment she laid eyes on me. Maybe she didn't agree with an urchin like me getting expensive care at Raspberry Hill for free. That was probably why no more children were coming to Ward Fourteen. Kristin had said that Sister Emerentia made the decisions at Raspberry Hill. She must have decided that no more poor children should come, and that the only one already here should die.

Of course that's what was going on. I felt rather clever when I worked it out.

I know I should have told Dr Hagman or Sister Petronella, but I was feeling so very sick and talking was difficult. I tried a few times, but found myself dozing off before I could get to the point. Everything was so hazy, I barely knew whether I was awake or asleep.

Anyway, it didn't really matter if Sister Emerentia was trying to kill me. I had always known I would die sooner or later. It just seemed that it was going to come a bit sooner than I had expected. It wasn't necessarily a bad thing. Everybody back home had forgotten about me already. I knew this because they hadn't written me a single word of a letter. So it was probably just as well. Besides, I didn't want to go on living with this terrible pain in my chest.

The only thing niggling at me was that I hadn't got round to writing that will. And now I was too exhausted to write a single line.

Then the strangest thing happened: it all turned around! For two weeks I had just been getting sicker and sicker, then suddenly I began to feel better again. My lungs sounded healthier, my throat stopped hurting and I felt much more awake.

Everyone congratulated Dr Hagman. Dr Funck shook his hand, and the nurses even applauded. His method worked!

The doctor seemed almost as surprised as I was,

meanwhile Sister Emerentia looked as if she had swallowed a lemon. I don't know what had happened to her plan, but it seemed that she hadn't managed to swap out my medicine often enough to reverse Dr Hagman's cure.

I made up my mind to keep an even closer eye on Sister Emerentia. If I started getting worse again, I would tell Dr Hagman what I had seen. She was jeopardizing his important research with her secret brown glass bottle.

For the first time in weeks, I was allowed to go out again. Sister Petronella dressed me in so many layers of clothing that I walked bow-legged. Winter was coming. There was no snow yet, but the lake was covered in a thin layer of ice and the birch trees were completely bare.

There were no more rich ladies lying out on the porch. They had all gone home when the autumn sun disappeared and the cold weather came. There were still a handful of other patients at Raspberry Hill, but it didn't seem like they were allowed to go out. Maybe they were all suffering as badly as I had been before. Or Dr Funck had gone around with his nasty gas syringe again.

I had the grounds to myself that morning. I moved very slowly because I was weak after lying in bed for so long. At least I wasn't cold, thanks to all the layers Sister Petronella had piled on me. I was almost a bit too warm as I shuffled along.

A squirrel scurried past. It was very beautiful, if indeed a squirrel can be described as beautiful. This one had such lovely fur and bright eyes. Its russet tail had a few touches of grey. It stopped and stared at me. Then it disappeared into a pine tree.

Once Ellen had tried to catch a squirrel and tame it, but no such luck. The squirrel probably didn't realize it had been captured, thinking it had just been invited to dinner in the woodshed before it merrily scuttled back to Brunnsparken. Ellen is a real animal lover, and if she is going to become a circus rider one day, she should probably start practising now.

The only horses we know are the two brewery horses that live in a stable near Saluhallen. They're not exactly graceful circus horses, but Ellen loves them. She scampers off to the brewery practically every day, sits on the fence and scratches the horses between the ears. They are very good horses. The brewers are kind to her too, and Ellen is such an adorable child that they usually let her stay. They shoo Lars, Olle and me away if we ever get too close to the fence. Erik is as fond of animals as Ellen is, but I think he would rather have that monkey than a horse or a squirrel.

It took me several minutes to walk down the steps to the lake. The question was whether I would be able to get back up again, but I supposed Sister Petronella would come out looking for me sooner or later and help me back inside.

I walked to the beautiful little lakeside pavilion. Just below it was a bench overlooking the water. By the time I realized there was someone sitting on the bench, it was too late. It was someone I would really rather not see, but I was too weak to run away.

When she turned her eerie white eyes toward me, I was so scared that I almost screamed.

But the old woman only said:

"Ah, still alive then, the poor child. I'm pleased."

When I didn't respond, she continued.

"You've no reason to fear me, dear girl. Come and sit on the bench with me a minute."

I hesitated. The old woman sounded kind, but something about her still made me think of the witches in old fairy tales. Was she going to lure me to her gingerbread house in the woods and eat me?

But in the end I did go and sit down on the farthest edge of the bench.

We sat quietly for a while. Then the old woman lifted her hand and pointed across the lake.

"See that smoke over there? It's coming from a chimney."

"Yes," I said.

Of course I saw the smoke, but no houses. On the other side of the lake nothing could be seen but woodland.

"There are several houses over there, and a farm. If I ever needed to run away from Raspberry Hill, that's where I would go."

"Why would you want to run away from Raspberry Hill?" I asked.

She laughed. A croaky little witch-cackle.

"No, *I* don't need to run away. I just think it might be worth bearing in mind. There's help on the other side of the lake."

I had no idea what she was talking about. Did she know something? Did she know that Sister Emerentia had tried to poison me? Did I dare ask her?

"There are wicked forces at work here at Raspberry Hill," the old woman continued. She sounded like she was mainly talking to herself. "As long as he is here, poor children will suffer."

"Who?" I whispered but she didn't seem to hear me.

"Do you know what I saw the other night with my own eyes? A light. A lamp shining in that wing where it all started. In the middle of the night he walks around there and continues forging his evil plans. He is the devil himself."

She spat out this last sentence and looked so utterly hideous that I leapt to my feet.

"I think I should go inside now."

The old woman stood up as well and called after me.

"Remember what I said! If he tries to take you to the East Wing, run as fast as you can! Go around the lake to safety! It's your only chance..."

I walked away as quickly as I could and didn't look back.

I had horrible nightmares that night. I dreamt I was locked in the lift and everything was burning. Sister Emerentia was standing close by and just watching me calmly, without helping. The old woman with the white eyes was laughing her hoarse cackle and

I cried out for Mama. I woke up with a jerk and sat up straight in bed. I think I was still screaming.

Ruben was sitting on the window sill.

"Nightmare?" he asked calmly.

"Where... where have you been?"

"Nowhere. Here and there."

"But not in Ward Twenty-three!"

"No. Not there exactly."

"But why did you say that you came from that ward?"

"Because it's the truth, of course."

"Ruben... Sister Emerentia is trying to kill me."

Ruben was taken aback, then he began to laugh. Dry, joyless laughter.

"Of course she isn't."

"I've seen her myself, switching my medicine!"

"How?"

"When Dr Hagman isn't looking, she takes an identical bottle out of her apron and hands it to him instead."

Ruben sighed deeply and shook his head.

"Think about it, Stina. When did you start getting better again? Was it before or after you saw Sister Emerentia switch your medicine?"

I thought about it.

"I got better afterwards... but..."

"There you go then."

"But Ruben, why would she?..."

"I only have time to say one more thing. You'll be safe at Raspberry Hill as long as Sister Emerentia is here. Do you understand?"

"But..."

"I have to go now. Good night."

"Ruben... are you real?"

No answer. I was alone in the dorm. And I hadn't heard the door open or close.

# 13

# The Staircase

S now came. I woke up one morning and was almost dazzled by the sight of it. The sky was white, the treetops were white and the whole lake was covered in snow. It was beautiful but made me melancholy.

It got me thinking about the people back home. Had it snowed on Sjömansgatan too? If it had, they would probably make a big snow pile in the middle of the courtyard for the children to climb on and dig holes in.

Once I beat Olle, Edith and even Ralf, the strong boy from the next building, playing king of the hill! I was only six years old at the time so I don't know how I did it. Somehow Ralf lost his balance and took

Olle down with him, and Edith was so gobsmacked that she was easily defeated. I will never forget the feeling of standing up there at the top of the pile with all the other kids looking up at me and shouting, "Stina won! Stina is king of the hill!" And down on the ground Olle, Edith and Ralf were all lying in a big pile looking sheepish.

I had written four letters home and not got a single one back, even though I had written the address of the sanatorium on the envelope in very neat letters.

It was probably as I suspected. They had simply forgotten about me. It was just as well.

It was also getting harder and harder to remember what Mama looked like. I often looked at the photograph of Mama and Papa, but Mama is so young and serious in it. Nothing like the mother who sat by the stove knitting me a cardigan. But no matter how much I closed my eyes and concentrated, I couldn't picture her face. It was sad.

At this time I wasn't better nor was I worse. In any case, it was clear that the fresh air at Raspberry Hill wasn't a miracle cure, so sometimes I hoped that they would just send me home again. But at the same time I was afraid that my family wouldn't want me back, coughing and infectious.

Sjömansgatan felt very far away. Almost like a different lifetime. Maybe this was my real life, here at Raspberry Hill.

I didn't know which way was up any more. Was I sick or healthy? Was Sister Emerentia good or evil? Where did Ruben live? And what was that witch trying to warn me about? Was it Dr Funck taking me to the East Wing to prick my lungs with his gas needle? No, it couldn't be!

The snow kept all the patients indoors. I had to content myself with climbing on the windowsill and looking out. It was a long time before I saw an actual living person from my window and even then it was only Mrs Hagman going down to the chief doctor's house on a kicksled.

Kicksleds are so much fun! One of the neighbourhood women back home has one, but I was only ever allowed to try it once. Edith and I took turns sitting and standing. Edith's legs were stronger than mine, and she got up to such a tremendous speed that I thought my ears might blow off. Luckily they didn't, but oh how fun it was to feel butterflies in my stomach.

Mrs Hagman was a lucky so-and-so to have her own kicksled.

A little later, a snow plough came up the hill, pulled by two large brown horses. And then I saw a cheering sight: a young woman sitting next to the driver. She saw me in the window and waved. It was Kristin! I waved back. I hoped she would come up and visit me.

I waited for Kristin for several hours, listening out for the clatter of her buckets. I dozed off while I was waiting, and in my half-asleep state thought I heard someone riding in the lift. The squeaking and scraping sounds reached all the way to Ward Fourteen.

Finally Kristin came. She claimed to have scrubbed every floor in the whole building. She was all sweaty and flushed.

"There's another little girl on the floor below, did you know that?" Kristin asked merrily as she scrubbed the floor underneath my bed.

"No, I didn't!"

"She looks very ill. Came in a very posh motor car a few hours ago. That's why they had to hurry my father here to plough a path up to the front door, so the car could get through..."

"Is the girl's name Esmeralda?" I asked.

"How should I know? I'm not the type to go about eavesdropping."

Sure, I thought. Kristin was *exactly* the type to go about eavesdropping. And I was glad she was—she knew so many interesting things. But I knew a thing or two myself.

"Esmeralda has a bad heart," I said, and was pleased to see Kristin's ears prick up.

"Does she? What's she doing at Raspberry Hill then? They only treat lung disease here, don't they?"

"I know, it's strange," I admitted. "But she does have a bad heart, she told me herself."

"Well, she looked very sick at any rate, poor mite."

I wondered whether Esmeralda knew that she was going to die soon as well. Was she as used to the idea as I was?

"Oof, I'd better fetch some fresh water," said Kristin. "Back soon!"

Off she went, lugging her two slopping buckets, and propping the door open with a chair. I heard her clattering all the way down the corridor.

Then I heard another sound. Footsteps and voices in the corridor. A man and a woman were approaching. They were speaking quietly in hissing voices and both sounded angry. I couldn't make out exactly what they were saying until the woman raised her voice and I recognized her as Sister Emerentia. But I had never heard her speak like this before, she was usually so cold and formal. Now she was almost shouting.

"I absolutely cannot condone this!" she said. "It is criminal! And utterly inhumane!"

The man's voice responded saying something I couldn't hear.

"I've warned you. I don't see that I have any choice but to call the police right away!" said Sister Emerentia.

Their steps faded into the distance. It sounded like Sister Emerentia and the man had turned around and gone back towards the stairs. I was lying in my bed, stiff as a rod, when Kristin came back.

"Did you hear the argument?" I asked.

"What argument?" said Kristin.

Just then there came a terrible scream. Kristin dropped both her buckets and water poured all over the floor. But there was no time to think about that. I leapt out of bed and together we rushed out of the dorm and down the corridor towards the stairs in the middle of the sanatorium, where the scream had come from. Someone was still screaming. Screaming and screaming and screaming.

Kristin got to the main staircase before I did, and when she leant over the railing and looked down, she started screaming too.

The screaming downstairs was coming from Sister Ingeborg. She was standing on the stone tiles of the ground floor with her face in her hands, wailing. Patients and nurses came rushing in from all the corridors and floors to see what was going on. The banister was so high that I had to climb down a few steps to be able to see what was happening.

Someone was lying on the floor near Sister Ingeborg. Someone dressed in white from head to toe. Someone whose bun had come loose as she had fallen down the stairs, surrounding her chalk-white face with long dark hair. Her arms and legs were splayed at unnatural angles, like a rag doll. It was Sister Emerentia.

# 14

# Fear

I had been living in Raspberry Hill sanatorium for several months. I'd made friends with a strange boy who appeared in my dormitory while I slept and met a white-eyed old woman who said I was in grave danger.

I'd believed I was being poisoned, and I'd been told that many people had lost their lives here in a terrible fire.

Yet I had never been genuinely afraid. Until now.

It was so strange, when I first came to Raspberry Hill I was ready to die. Death had seemed inevitable. Dying young was my destiny, just as Edith's destiny was to sell hats and Olle's was to sail the seas.

Of course, on occasion I had wondered what would

happen after I coughed my final cough and breathed my final breath. Would I see Papa again? Would I go to heaven, like they said in church? Then again, it seemed pretty pointless to dwell on these things in advance. I would find out soon enough.

But now that death seemed so close, I was scared. I lay in my bed in Ward Fourteen and felt fear consume all other thoughts. I was afraid of everything! Of death and how much it would hurt when it came. Of Raspberry Hill. Of the doctors and nurses. The bathtub, the mangle, the mortuary.

I think it was the scream that changed everything. I heard it in my mind over and over. Not Sister Ingeborg's scream. The first one. Sister Emerentia's scream as she plunged down the stairs. The sound of a person staring death in the face.

Would I scream like that when my time came?

Ruben's words also echoed in my ears. That I would be safe as long as Sister Emerentia was at Raspberry Hill. Now she was gone.

I didn't know if Sister Emerentia was dead or alive. Dr Funck had been first on the scene and made sure Sister Emerentia was put in an ambulance straight away. It seemed strange to me that an injured person would be taken *away* from a hospital, but Sister

Petronella explained that Raspberry Hill doesn't have the right kind of medical equipment to help someone who has fallen down a flight of stairs.

Sister Petronella said that Dr Funck had gone with her in the ambulance. She was crying as she told me. All the nurses were crying as they helped Kristin dry the floor in my room. They couldn't believe how awful it was that Sister Emerentia had tripped on the very same stairs they all used many times a day. Even though she always walked with such a straight back, so collected, never rushing or dragging her heels.

I, on the other hand, was certain that Sister Emerentia had not tripped on the stairs at all. Someone had pushed her. Probably the person she had been arguing with in the corridor outside Ward Fourteen. But I didn't tell the nurses. They were frightened enough as it was. And if it was Dr Funck, it was already too late. He had gone with her in the ambulance...

All patients were told to stay in our rooms that night and only call for help in an emergency. Sister Emerentia, Dr Funck and the two ambulance drivers were out, so there weren't many people on site to care for us.

When night fell, it was even quieter than usual. I thought I heard someone crying in the distance, but the sound stopped before long.

The moon was shining in through my window, straight in my face, but I didn't turn my head. I couldn't sleep anyway, so the moon could dazzle me as much as it wanted. I got the feeling this might be my last night alive. I didn't want to waste it sleeping.

I was still wide awake when I heard footsteps in the corridor a few hours later. Hurried steps coming closer and closer. Heels clacking loudly on the floor tiles. It didn't sound like one of the nurses on the night round. They usually walked as quietly as possible and wore soft-soled shoes.

The door to my room opened and someone came in. The moon cast a streak of light across the door and I caught a glimpse of who it was. Mrs Hagman. She rarely came up to the second floor. Maybe she was helping with the night round because all the nurses were so shaken up?

I assumed I would be scolded if she saw that I was awake so I pretended to be asleep. I heard Mrs Hagman fiddle with something and then it became quiet. I opened my eyes just a crack to see what she was doing.

In that moment I felt a sting in my arm. It hurt so badly that I went to scream, but quick as a flash Mrs Hagman clamped her hand over my mouth.

"Now, don't struggle. It was just a little prick. You won't feel any pain at all once the anaesthetic sets in."

To my horror, I could feel something spreading through my body. Paralysing me. Stopping me from being able to make a sound.

Mrs Hagman removed her hand, rolled out a wheelchair and lifted me out of bed. She was surprisingly strong.

I managed to find my voice. I didn't have the strength to scream, but I could whisper.

"Cardigan. Photograph."

"What?"

"I want my cardigan and the photograph of my parents. On the chest of drawers."

It was strange, even though I had been lying in bed terrified for so long, I suddenly felt stubborn.

It was happening. I was going to die tonight. I understood that. But I wanted to have some say about how it would happen. I wanted the scent of my mother and to see her face as I fell asleep. That would make it just a little better. It wasn't a lot to ask, was it?

Mrs Hagman looked puzzled, but she wrapped me in my cardigan and put the photograph on my lap.

Then she rolled me away.

The corridors were deserted and the night nurse's room was empty. We passed the lift and the main stairs and continued through corridor after corridor on the second floor. I was completely limp and almost fell forward several times, but Mrs Hagman pulled me back each time.

Eventually we came to a staircase. Someone was waiting for us. I recognized his silhouette and sideburns.

It was Dr Hagman.

He had no kind words for me this time. No 'little friend' or 'little miss'. He just picked me up and started carrying me down the stairs.

# 15

# Two Hearts

I had already figured out where we were going and, sure enough, we soon came to the corridor where I had hidden in the recess of a doorway some weeks before. Mrs Hagman unlocked the door in the glass wall and we entered the East Wing. As we started down the corridor I saw a light on in a room several doors along.

It was an operating theatre. Unlike everything else I had seen of the East Wing, this room was very clean and tidy. The floor was well scrubbed and the metal surfaces were polished to a sheen.

In the middle of the room was an operating table covered with a sheet. Dr Hagman laid me down on it gently. Then finally he looked at me and smiled his usual friendly smile.

"Good evening, Stina."

"Good evening, Dr Hagman," I replied politely.

I could speak again, but my voice came out as groggy and weak.

"Tonight is a big night, Stina."

"Am I going to?..."

"Tonight we are going to make medical history, you and I. You shall be famous, Stina!"

"What for?"

"Before I explain, I want you to try to remain calm. This isn't going to hurt."

That was good to hear.

"You'll have one more injection, of course, but the anaesthetic my wife gave you means it won't hurt in the least. This second injection will make you sleep very deeply."

"So deeply that I die?"

Dr Hagman didn't answer, he just kept smiling and started fiddling with something in a little trolley.

"Dr Hagman, may I ask you something?"

"Of course, little friend."

"Why are we doing this? Injections and operating

theatres in the middle of the night? Surely I'm going to die soon anyway?"

Dr Hagman's expression became hugely enthusiastic.

"Have you ever heard of a transplant?"

I shook my head. Some feeling had returned in my upper body, I noticed. Just enough for me to move my neck.

"It's like this: your lungs are in ruins. They can't hold out much longer, a week at the most. But your heart is healthy and strong. Can you turn your head to the right, little friend?"

I could. I saw a second operating table on the other side of the room. It looked like someone was lying on it! Someone about the same size as me, covered in a sheet.

Suddenly I realized how it all came together. It was crystal clear! How had I not put two and two together before?

"Dr Hagman, is that Esmeralda?"

The doctor was very taken aback.

"Do you know her?"

"She has a bad heart."

"She *had* a bad heart, poor thing. A heart that stopped beating just an hour ago."

"And now you want to... give her my heart?"

"Oh Stina, truly! How I wish that tuberculosis had never sunk its claws into you! Your sharp intellect could have been a great asset to the medical profession!"

"But how? Isn't she already dead?"

"I've been researching this matter for thirty years! And some years ago I successfully managed to transplant the heart of one piglet into another! I came very close to trying the same experiment with two little boys here at Raspberry Hill, but alas I was foiled. Just think how many lives could be saved if I succeed tonight."

I did my best to think about it.

"But not my life?"

Dr Hagman had started organizing things in his trolley again and answered without looking up at me.

"It is a pity. But you are destined to die in any case. Imagine if your heart could give Esmeralda a new chance at life. Esmeralda's parents are very modern thinkers, and though they have already bid farewell to their daughter, deep down they are hoping that the transplant will be a success. And if it is, know that I'll make sure your name appears in all the medical articles and reports."

"Fancy that."

It was a lot to take in at once. I didn't much like the idea of Dr Hagman cutting out my heart when I was dead. But I'd be gone, so what did it really matter?

"But Dr Hagman, can you really do this?"

He hummed a little. Not 'The Lullaby Waltz' this time, something more sombre.

"It is a shame that it's all happening so suddenly. This wasn't my intention. I tried to plan your medication in such a way that the deterioration would be gradual. Unfortunately, there were some who chose to oppose me."

"Sister Emerentia? She gave me a different medicine, didn't she?"

"I'm afraid I can't answer that, little friend. Is there anything I can do for you, Stina? To make this as pleasant as possible?"

I thought for a moment.

"Yes please, Dr Hagman. I'd like it if you could put the photograph of my parents somewhere I can see it when I get the injection."

"But of course."

Dr Hagman propped the photograph up carefully against a glass bottle on another small trolley to the left of my head.

Mrs Hagman reappeared. She had put on a white coat and laid some objects out on a small tray that she placed on the trolley with the photograph.

"I am ready, Georg," she said.

"Excellent, let us begin..."

A bell rang loud and clear somewhere in the sanatorium. Dr Hagman cursed.

"What the hell is that? A patient calling for help?"

"That's what it sounds like, Georg."

"And the night nurse?"

"Sister Ingeborg is under sedation, as we agreed. I put opium in her tea. She won't stir before morning."

"Then one of us has to go and see what the patient wants. Otherwise we risk the other patients waking up and disturbing us in the middle of the operation. This must not happen again."

"Shall I?..."

"No, Gertrud, I'll go."

Dr Hagman marched out of the room, muttering to himself. Mrs Hagman looked at me. She almost seemed nervous. I attempted a weak smile to show her that I wasn't sad or scared, but that just made her look even more uncomfortable.

"I must fetch more ether..." she mumbled and

disappeared through a smaller door that must have led to some sort of storeroom.

I was left alone. Apart from Esmeralda of course, but she was dead.

"You do know that they're lying, right?" a boy's voice suddenly shouted.

Ruben was standing at the end of the operating table looking furious.

"About what?" I whispered back so that Mrs Hagman wouldn't hear.

"You're not dying. You're getting better. Sister Emerentia has been giving you the right medicine for weeks now. She figured out Dr Hagman's plans. That's why he pushed her down the stairs."

"How do you know?"

"How do you think? Because he did the same thing to me, of course!"

Ruben unbuttoned his nightshirt to reveal a long red scar just above his heart.

"He tried to give my heart to another boy. We were poor kids with bad lungs and our parents were mostly just grateful not to have to worry about us. We were all like that in Ward Twenty-three, poor kids from big families. They forgot about us."

"Just like my family..."

"Your mother hasn't forgotten about you, Stina. She's been writing every week. To you and to Dr Hagman."

"She has?"

"Mrs Hagman burns the letters in the stove as soon as they come. They want you to think that your family has forgotten you. But it's not true. Do you really want to die, Stina?"

I let out a heavy sigh.

"Yes, I do."

"I don't believe you. Why die if you don't have to? I didn't get a choice, but you do!"

He was so angry that his face had turned even whiter than usual.

"How do you think this makes us feel? All the kids who died on Hagman's operating table or in the fire? You lying here refusing to fight, just to be contrary, because you've given up?"

Now I started to get angry too.

"I don't have a choice either! I can't even move!"

"Can't you? Try!"

I let out an exasperated sigh and tried to raise my right hand. I didn't think it would work, but to my amazement it rose straight up in the air.

"There, you see," said Ruben.

"So what? I can wave my hand, what good is that to me?"

Ruben smiled a crooked little smile and went over to the trolley where Mrs Hagman had put down her tray. I shuddered when I turned my head and saw what was on it. Knives. Small but very sharp. A metal bowl. Some folded linen towels. And two large syringes.

I bit my lip. The tools to kill me were right before my eyes. The bowl, was that where they were going to put my heart? And that would be that. No turning back once it was done.

What if Ruben was telling the truth? What if Mama hadn't forgotten me? What if she missed me and was worried? And what if I wasn't dying after all, if maybe I could get better?...

"Here's what you could do..." said Ruben, then he leant forward and whispered.

I listened carefully to every word.

# 16

# The Ice

Ruben was right.

It was my duty to try to get away. I probably wouldn't make it, but the most important thing was not to give up.

I was sorry for Esmeralda, of course. Nothing would change the fact that she was dead. And sorry for her parents, sitting somewhere in the sanatorium and crying, hoping that Dr Hagman could wake her up again.

Still, it wasn't my fault Esmeralda was dead. It wasn't fair for us both to die just because Dr Hagman wanted to make medical history.

And imagine if what Ruben had said was true? That I really was getting better. That maybe I could be cured. I had never dared dream that I might have a healthy life ahead of me.

A healthy child who goes to school, plays king of the hill and fetches drinking water from the pump. And then one fine day an adult who writes articles for the newspaper, maybe gets married and has children of her own. I hadn't allowed myself to even think such things for a long time.

If there was even the slightest chance, shouldn't I take it?

By the time Mrs Hagman returned, Ruben had disappeared. I couldn't see him but I could sense that he was hiding in the darkness somewhere, watching.

In fact, I got the feeling that he wasn't the only one watching me and Mrs Hagman. Maybe all the poor sick children who had lost their lives at Raspberry Hill because Dr Hagman wanted to be a world-famous surgeon had come to watch me from the shadows. That's what it felt like. And that they were all crossing their fingers for me. They made me feel strong and almost brave.

Mrs Hagman held a small glass bottle in each hand as she approached the operating table. She glanced at me and I smiled at her again. Then she looked away to put the bottles down on the trolley.

"What on earth..." she said when she noticed that one of the syringes was gone.

It was in my hand. I raised it high, plunged the needle into Mrs Hagman's buttock and squeezed all the fluid into her body.

She let out a yelp and fell forward, dragging the trolley down with her as she fell. She looked at me, her eyes wide open in terror, then floundered on the floor for a few moments before going still. It was horrible to watch.

"Ruben!" I shouted. "I haven't killed her, have I?"

It dawned on me that what I was doing might cost someone their life. Mrs Hagman had intended to kill me first, of course, but that didn't make it right!

Ruben appeared by my side.

"She's fine. The dose in the syringe would kill a small, sickly child, but not a healthy, full-grown woman. She'll be paralysed for a while. Hurry now before the doctor comes back."

I had regained control of my arms, but my legs were still as heavy as logs. The only way I could get down from the table was to use my arms to roll sideways and fall to the floor with a crash.

"Are you OK?" I heard Ruben ask.

"No," I whimpered.

I had landed on my face. If I lived to see the morning, I would have a terrible bruise all over my left cheek. The overturned trolley had fallen away from me and the other syringe had rolled almost all the way to where Esmeralda lay. I tried not to look at Mrs Hagman. Her face had frozen in a ghastly expression as if she were screaming for her life.

I crawled forward slowly. I wouldn't get far this way. I hoped that the patient who had called Dr Hagman was far away at the other end of the sanatorium so he wouldn't return for a long time. Finally I managed to reach the syringe with my fingers. Dear me, the needle was huge.

"Hurry up, Stina," Ruben whispered behind me.

Easy for him to say. The only thing I hated more than needles was fire. And now I was expected to stick this great big needle into myself. No, maybe it would be better to let myself be killed after all...

I started to cry. It was all too awful and so unfair. What had I done to deserve this?

I saw something lying on the floor next to me. It was the photograph of my parents. I picked it up and cried some more.

Mama and Papa looked up at me with grave expressions. They were so young and beautiful. Soon they would marry and have six children. And then fate would separate them. Did they know that somehow? Could that be why they looked so serious? For the first time, it seemed that they were really looking straight at me from the photo. Their sombre expressions spoke to me.

Time to steel yourself, Stina.

Do what you must do.

I gritted my teeth and picked up the syringe, the one that Dr Hagman was going to stick into Esmeralda's lifeless body to give her a new jolt of life. I scrunched up my eyes and jabbed it deep into my own skinny thigh instead. It was a dreadful thing to do, but it didn't hurt all that much. Dr Hagman had been telling the truth that time. The anaesthetic meant I could barely feel the syringe.

What happened next was incredible. My whole body became very hot. Then cold, then hot again. My heart started pounding at an unbelievable rate. It really was a good strong heart, just like the doctor had said. A good enough heart to be put into the chest of a rich little girl. But this heart belonged to Stina, the little ragamuffin from Sjömansgatan, and no one else. And I wasn't about to let it be taken away from me just like that.

I got up effortlessly. Strangely enough, I felt taller than usual. I could feel the blood flowing around my body, I felt strong and fast. My face didn't even hurt any more.

"Run, Stina!" said Ruben from somewhere in the shadows.

And I ran.

Sometimes I have dreams where I can run as fast and as far as I want without getting the slightest bit tired. But then I always wake up as the same weak Stina who can barely walk without getting out of breath.

This was just like one of those dreams, but for real.

Ruben was running just ahead of me, showing me where to go.

"This way, over here," he called and I followed him.

Suddenly I heard a roar behind me. It was coming from a man. Dr Hagman must have come back and found his wife on the floor. I hoped Ruben knew where he was going, else we might come to a dead end...

He led me to a window with a gap where a pane had come loose. Cold air blew through. The gap wasn't very big, but then again neither was I. Perhaps I could squeeze through it if I held my breath...

"Watch out for broken glass," Ruben whispered.

I tried to be careful but still managed to cut myself along one arm. But there was no time to think about that.

I was outside! The window wasn't too high above the ground so I didn't hurt myself when I landed in the snow.

Ruben stayed inside. I saw his white face through the gap in the window.

"Run, Stina!" he said again.

"What about you?"

"I have to stay here. Run!"

I was barefoot and the cold snow felt like a million needles pricking my feet. But that couldn't be helped.

I stumbled and staggered, tripped and struggled. I didn't dare look back, terrified that I might see Dr Hagman coming after me, his eyes ablaze, raising another deadly syringe. I kept looking ahead, ahead, ahead.

There was no use trying to hide, my footprints in the snow would show exactly where I had gone. I didn't dare call for help either. The patients in the sanatorium might hear me, but could they do anything? And would they believe me over Dr Hagman?

My only option was to get away, no matter what.

I was almost at the lake, right next to the chief doctor's house. And there, by the gate, was a kick-sled! A quality sled painted red—it was the one Mrs Hagman used.

The sled was heavy and I cut my leg on one of the runners when I tried to pull it free. But I managed to get it out onto the frozen lake. Luckily, it had small footrests on the runners, otherwise I probably wouldn't have been able to stand on them without shoes. I took a run up before placing one foot on one side and pushing off with the other.

The kicksled was too big for me really, but I had the elixir of life pumping through my veins and was fighting for survival.

It would have been pitch-black on the lake if it hadn't been for the moonlight. I tried to remember roughly where the lady with the white eyes had pointed. Where were those houses where she'd said I could get help? It was a long way to the other side of the lake. Would I make it? And would the ice hold?...

"Damn brat! Stop this instant!"

My blood ran cold when I heard Dr Hagman's furious bellow behind me. How close was he?

I glanced over my shoulder and screamed in horror. He wasn't far at all! He was going to catch me! He was an adult, he was healthy and he had shoes on! I was done for!

Tears welled up in my eyes and my nose began to run as I strained to summon the last of my strength. I knew it was in vain, but I was determined to fight to the last. I owed it to Ruben and the others. As long as I had the slightest chance, I would keep fighting.

"I'm going to kill you, you little wretch."

I kicked and kicked, cried and sobbed. I could taste blood in my mouth, probably from coughing too hard and opening old wounds in my throat. I could barely see anything through my tears. I had no idea how far it was to the other side. Any moment now I would feel the furious doctor's heavy fist on my shoulder and it would all be over.

The doctor yelled again behind me, but differently this time. It was a cry of surprise. And terror. Then there was a strange cracking sound that turned into a crash and a splash. Then silence. All I could hear were my own gasps and the whistling sound of the sled's runners cutting through the snow. I didn't dare stop but managed to muster the courage to turn my head to look back.

Dr Hagman had disappeared. Behind me instead was a large black hole in the ice.

I slowed down. The ice crackled ominously under my feet.

The lake had devoured the doctor and it could just as easily take me with him. I definitely wasn't safe yet.

I wiped my tears with the sleeve of my cardigan and looked around. I had to get to land. But which direction was the quickest and safest choice? What would happen if I went back to the sanatorium? Would more dangers be waiting for me? Were other people in on Dr Hagman's plan?

The ice creaked again beneath me. Staying still was dangerous, I needed to keep moving. But which way?

"Ruben!" I cried helplessly. "Ruben! Where should I go?"

And in that very moment, as if by miracle, I saw a light on the shore. No, two lights! Was it Ruben signalling to me which direction to go? No, it was a motor car driving towards the sanatorium.

Who was it? Friend or foe?

There was nothing else for it—they were my only hope.

I set off again. I kicked, kicked, kicked, called for help and tried to wave one arm while clinging to the kicksled with the other.

*Ruben, Ruben, help me, save me.*

*Papa Paul, Grandma Josefa and all the angels in heaven.*

*Let whoever is coming here be kind.*

*Let me make it to land.*

*Let me continue to live!*

*I want to live! Do you hear? I want to live!*

The car stopped. Three people got out. One of them was about to start running towards me, but they were held back by someone else. Which was the right thing to do. The ice might not hold their weight.

I let go of the kicksled and stumbled the last stretch on foot, blinded by tears.

I recognized the woman who was trying to run towards me. I could hear her calling my name. Now I was crying more than ever.

It was Mama.

# 17

# The Most Beautiful Place

I can hardly believe I once told Kristin that Sjömansgatan wasn't a beautiful place. How could I have been so wrong?

Sjömansgatan is the most beautiful place in the world! And most beautiful of all was our little kitchen that first evening after Dr Lundin had deemed me thawed out enough to go home. We all sat in front of the fire: my brothers, my sisters, Mama and me. We huddled together in a big pile, laughing and crying in turn. My siblings asked me to tell them all about what had happened and I tried to, several times, but the words wouldn't come out. I could only manage snippets of stories that didn't make sense and eventually I had to give up. It could wait. Even

Olle sniffed and sobbed but I thought better than to make fun of him.

And all the letters they had written! Every single week, they wrote. Every evening they had looked at my empty bed in the kitchen and cried and wondered how I was and if I was even still alive.

Mama had saved up to send expensive telegrams to Raspberry Hill and even tried to call on the telephone, but never got an answer.

Of all the letters I had written, only one had reached them! The hardest one to write, the one saying I was getting worse and expected to die soon. The one I had put in my drawer and forgotten to give to the nurses the next morning.

I guess Sister Emerentia must have posted it before Mrs Hagman got the chance to burn it.

Mama had been beside herself when she read it and tried desperately to raise money for a train ticket to get to the sanatorium, but in vain.

Not long after, a man had come to pay Mama a visit. He was the editor of a daily newspaper and was investigating rumours about a certain Dr Georg Hagman.

His name was Mr Forsman, and he had heard people say that the fire at Raspberry Hill was no accident. When the editor began to investigate the matter, he realized that there were a lot of children who had gone to the sanatorium for treatment and never came home again. And all of them were from poor families with lots of siblings.

Editor Forsman thought it was strange that so many poor children could afford to stay in such an expensive sanatorium, and even though tuberculosis is a terrible disease indeed, it still seemed strange that not a single one of these children got better and came home.

The editor wanted to know if there was any truth behind the rumours and managed to find out that Mama had a child at Raspberry Hill at the time.

He was the one who had stopped Mama from running out onto the ice. The third person in the car was a police officer.

When Sister Emerentia was taken to the emergency room it caused quite a stir and Editor Forsman decided to take Mama to Raspberry Hill and alert the police.

Yes, Sister Emerentia. She survived! She broke both legs and one arm and suffered concussion from the fall, but as soon as she opened her eyes she demanded to speak to the chief of police and tell him everything she knew about Dr and Mrs Hagman. Sister Emerentia would make a full recovery, said Editor Forsman. I was very happy to hear it.

Mrs Hagman lived too. She was in police custody, to be charged with murder. How many murders was still unclear.

Dr Hagman hadn't been found.

Poor Dr Lundin was mortified. He was the one who had arranged for me to go to Raspberry Hill. He had known Dr Hagman ever since they studied medicine together and never dreamt that his old friend would put me in any kind of danger. He must have apologized at least a dozen times, though I forgave him straight away. Mama was the one who needed twelve apologies before she could forgive him.

Dr Lundin said it was a miracle that my toes hadn't frozen off when I was sledding across the frozen lake. It must have been thanks to Dr Hagman's elixir of life. It turned out to be a very good injection that I gave myself! Hopefully the doctor wrote down the recipe for the elixir somewhere before he got swallowed up by the lake.

Of course I became very weak after that night on the ice, but Dr Lundin watched over me at home in my mama's own kitchen. She and I both refused to follow his advice to send me to another hospital.

Slowly, I got better.

Oh yes, I forgot to mention Mrs Frostmo! She's very important too! The old lady with the white eyes, or the witch, as I called her.

She was the one who had made the biggest fuss to Editor Forsman. She had written letter after letter to the newspaper explaining that terrible things were going on at Raspberry Hill Sanatorium. She wasn't a patient, as I had thought, but lived in a cabin in the woods some distance away and came to the sanatorium grounds for walks. She had noticed that there were fewer and fewer children playing in the gardens, and more and more crosses appearing outside the mortuary. But no one believed her, except Editor Forsman. Mrs Frostmo was also the one who went to the village to send a telegram to the editor when the ambulance drove away with Sister Emerentia.

Maybe Mrs Frostmo really is a witch who lives in a hut in the woods. But if she is, she must be a very good witch.

I hope to thank her someday. And apologize for thinking she was a witch.

# 18

# Moving On

It was spring when I went back to Raspberry Hill. Editor Forsman took me and Mama, and a photographer from the newspaper came too. Editor Forsman had decided he was going to write one last article about Raspberry Hill, even though he had already won a journalism prize for his revelations about the Hagmans. This last article would mostly be about me and how I was getting along a few months later.

So, how was I getting along? Just great! Dr Lundin said I was back to health, thanks in large part to all the clean air and good food, as well as the medicine that Sister Emerentia had given me in secret. I continued taking it until I didn't need it any more.

How could we afford such an expensive medicine? Well, truth be known, Stina from Sjömansgatan isn't so wretchedly poor any more.

Esmeralda's parents paid for my care. They had also been fooled by Dr Hagman. He had told them that their daughter was going to receive the heart of someone who had died of natural causes, a consumptive child who couldn't be cured. Not a child who was going to be murdered with a giant syringe.

It turned out that Esmeralda's father was a member of parliament. It was very important to him that the matter was handled "dispassionately and discreetly", as he put it. He wanted to give me a lot of money as compensation for all the pain and suffering, and to avoid a scandal.

Mama was furious when he said this, saying that the lives of two little girls was nothing to be discreet about, and she ought to tell the whole world what the Hagmans had been trying to do. Mama shouted that our silence was not for sale. Well said, I thought.

I don't really know how they resolved it because they refused to discuss it in front of me. But in the end, Esmeralda's father paid for my medical care and set me up with a bank account filled with money! Mama made sure I won't be allowed to touch it until I'm grown up though. And even then it is supposed to go on a proper education, because I've been blessed with a bright mind, Mama says.

Fine by me. I know exactly what I want to be. I'm going to be a doctor. One that makes young children better. And not the other way around, like Dr Hagman.

Raspberry Hill Sanatorium had been shut down again. No rich ladies wanted to go there any more, and they couldn't find staff either. The once so mighty grey stone facade looked rather shabby in the spring sun and the building was empty and deserted. I thought it looked like it had shrunk, but of course that was impossible.

I wondered what had happened to Sister Petronella, Sister Ingeborg and the others. I hoped they had got jobs at other hospitals and were doing well. And that Kristin would go to the nursing institute in the autumn.

The two doctors' houses were empty too. Dr Funck had moved abroad, according to Editor Forsman. I glanced down at the white pavilion and shuddered. That was where Dr Hagman's body had finally floated ashore when the ice broke up. Right next to the bench where Mrs Frostmo and I had sat last autumn.

Editor Forsman and I wandered around for a while. He asked me questions and I tried to give wise, insightful answers.

The photographer took some pictures of me and Mama in front of the sanatorium. It wasn't the first time I had been photographed. They had already taken a picture of me for the first article, but that one didn't come out very well because my face was all bruised and swollen after falling off the operating table before I escaped. Olle almost laughed himself sick when that picture appeared in the newspaper.

"Well, Stina, you're no Greta Garbo, but you have other strengths..."

This time I hoped the picture would come out better.

When we came to the mortuary I asked to be left alone for a few minutes. Mama, the photographer and the editor started walking back to the car as I opened the gate and walked into the small cemetery.

I had to search awhile before I found him.

It was a simple little wooden cross that had gone

crooked. *Ruben Alexander Wiik 1915–1923* was written on the cross. I took the small bouquet of violets I had bought from a flower stand in the town square. It was still beautiful, even though I had been holding it in my arms throughout the long drive. I laid it down by the cross and waited.

I didn't have to wait long.

"Hello," said Ruben.

He was sitting on the mortuary steps with that cheeky look on his face. He was smartly dressed, in grey shorts and a white shirt. I think he had tried to use a wet comb as well, but most of his fair hair still stuck out.

"Hello, Ruben," I said. "Do you like violets?"

"Sure I do. I don't think anyone has ever given me violets before. Thank you very much."

I sat down next to him on the step.

"You look healthy," he said.

"So do you."

"I've been waiting for you. I was hoping you'd come back."

"Here I am."

We sat in silence for a while. Ruben looked so nice in the sunshine. He was so pale he almost shone. More like an angel than a ghost, I thought.

A cuckoo called somewhere. A fly buzzed past. I cleared my throat.

"I wanted to thank you for saving my life," I said shyly.

It was such a very solemn thing to say.

"Ach," said Ruben, looking a little embarrassed. "You did most of it yourself."

"But I wouldn't have known what to do if you hadn't explained about the syringes. And shown me the way out of the East Wing."

"Sure."

We sat quietly a little longer.

"I feel sorry for Esmeralda," I said. "She never got a new heart."

"Don't think that. She never wanted your heart."

"How would you know?"

"She told me, of course."

"You spoke?"

"Oh sure. She was ready to die, she'd been waiting a long time. She was angry with her parents for hoping Dr Hagman would try to wake her up again instead of just letting her go. She wanted to move on..."

"Move on where?"

"Ah well, I don't know. Wherever all the other

kids have moved on to. Except me. I had to put things right here first."

"But now you're going..."

"I think it's time now. How do I look?"

I studied him. He seemed different. He wasn't smiling his sly little smile, his expression was serious and rather nervous.

"Very smart."

"Why thank you. You know what, Stina?"

"What?"

"It wasn't easy convincing you to go on living, so now I think it would be polite of you to keep on living until you're at least a hundred years old."

"I will, Ruben. I promise I'll try, anyway."

He smiled.

"Well then, Stina. Time to say goodbye."

Ruben stood up and bowed low. I got to my feet too and curtsied. When I looked up again, he was gone.

It struck me that I had forgotten yet again to ask Ruben the many questions I was so curious about. Like all that about moving on—where did people go? Was there a heavenly door somewhere? Was it a staircase up into the clouds? Or a long corridor with a light at the end like some people said? Where do we go?

But it was too late to ask questions. And I'll find out for myself when the time comes.

It will have to wait though.

My name is Stina and I am planning on living for at least another eighty-eight years!

AVAILABLE AND COMING SOON
FROM PUSHKIN CHILDREN'S BOOKS

We created Pushkin Children's Books to share tales from different languages and cultures with younger readers, and to open the door to the wide, colourful worlds these stories offer.

From picture books and adventure stories to fairy tales and classics, and from fifty-year-old bestsellers to current huge successes abroad, the books on the Pushkin Children's list reflect the very best stories from around the world, for our most discerning readers of all: children.

**THE MURDERER'S APE**
**SALLY JONES AND THE FALSE ROSE**
**THE LEGEND OF SALLY JONES**

*Jakob Wegelius*

**WHEN LIFE GIVES YOU MANGOES**
**IF YOU READ THIS**

*Kereen Getten*

**BOY 87**
**LOST**
**MELT**
**FAKE**

*Ele Fountain*